THE ORACLE OF THE MISSING DRYAD

an Alyson Bell novel

Sometimes the pages just write themselves... as though, the spirit of the wood still lives between the text, dancing between pages and weaving magic.

Alyson Bell meets a tree dryad who helps her on her latest adventure - that is, until the book the spirit is hiding in gets stolen. It's up to Alyson to travel through time to find her! She holds the key that unlocks both the past and the future, and her prophecy is discovered. Thus reveals...

THE ORACLE OF THE MISSING DRYAD

an Alyson Bell novel

Kristin Groulx

The Tenth Muse Books

This book is a work of fiction. Names, characters, businesses, organizations, places, events, and incidents either are the product of the author's imagination or are used fictitiously. Any resemblance to actual persons, living or dead, events, or locales is entirely coincidental.

The Oracle of the Missing Dryad

Copyright © 2009 by Kristin Groulx

ISBN 978-0-9811315-2-8

Published by The Tenth Muse Books

www.thetenthmusebooks.com

All rights reserved. No part of this publication may be reproduced, stored in a retrieval system, or transmitted in any form by any process – electronic, mechanical, photocopying, recording, or otherwise – without the prior written permission of the copyright owners, and from the publisher.

Copy Editor: Eric D. Goodman

Cover and Interior Design: Moonspinner Designs

Back cover: "Innocence" by Biljana Banchotova
www.BiljanaArt.com

This book is set in Garamond
Titles and embellishes: Lilith, Minya Nouvelle and 1942 Report

*This book is playful, but dark. 13+
It's not meant for those less than thirteen years of age, truly. Use your best judgment. Enjoy.*

DEDICATION

This book is dedicated to the children. They are the acorns, the seeds. They will carry the fruit of the next generation. They will grow into their own magnificence, laying the foundation and grounding roots where they stand. Our children are strong. Our children will grow old with many stories to tell, of the things they've seen and places they've been, and of those special souls that came into their lives at just the right time to leave their mark.

"I see my path, but I don't know where it leads. Not knowing is what inspires me to travel it." - Rosalia de Castro

Acknowledgements

I would like to say thank you to the following people: my husband François Groulx; my children Hallie, Josh & Julien, my parents John & Deborah Carter; All of the *Carter, Groulx & Peterson* clans… where would I be without my family… , sisters Mireille Johnson, Sylvie Groulx; my closest of spiritual friends, Chad & Deanna Lemieux, Rick Dhur, Marie Douville, Rahim Jetha, Monique Goguen, Michelle Budzinski, Marie Bergsma, Stephane Lebeau, Tracy Thillman, Annie Langlois, Chantelle Russell, Ami & Kyle Smith, Biljana Banchotova, Brad Johnson; friends that inspire Betsy Hawkins, Eileen Garde, Jackie Koshnick & Alison Wynne-Ryder, Scott Parker, Anne Rice, Barbara Niven, Victoria Parker, Michelle Gardner, Wendell Johnson, David Weitzman, Matthew Stapley, Richard Pearce, Ellie Crystal, Druanna Johnston, Anya Briggs; friends that are full of beauty Katherine Morrison, Ana Franchesca Rousseau Jenkins, Evonne de La Fuente, Zena Nesrallah, Elisa McBride, Melissa St. James, Marie-Claire Groulx; old friends from high school Bonnie Campbell, Jackie Culver, Sarah Kendziorski, Chris Pipkins, Tara Dawson, Reggie Carig, David Dunham, Kristy DuBeau, Junko Okamura, Melissa Parkhurst, Christine Raghianti, Nina Slagle, Larry Schlesinger, Scott Burton, Kasi Adams, Jennifer Hosfield, Scot Jones, Ryan O'Neil, Christian Varner, Dave C. Wyatt; old friends from college Annette Freeman, Mark Heisten, Matt Schneider, Anthony & Christy Graves, Glenn Kuhlman (in memory), Kathi Turner, Steven Garratt; photographer Kevin Russ who provided the cover photo of Ana; friends that love to write, J.D. Hobbes, Autumn Hiscock, Rob McLennan, Rob St. Martin, Eric D. Goodman, Brendan Myers, Karen Dales, Edain Duguay; friends that love to draw, Janet Liston Watkins, Bonni Nye; great friends Rae Lynn Beck, David Slater, Laurie Foster, Diamond Jim MacLeod, Jeremy Wrench, Kristina Mackay, Bill & Jennifer Flegg, Jennifer Spencer, Louis Gaal, Claire Faguy, Marc Duguay, Rose & Mitch McDermott, Gus Croteau, Morgan Blackbyrne, Laurie Stewart, Steffan Watkins, Sylvie Charbonneau, Conrad Alardus, Paula Sepp-Schultz, Holly Naughton, Pat Naughton, Rose Vitagliano, Teal Lundy, Vanessa Smith, Lynda Harder, Nancy Harder & George (in memory), Peggy Grant, Rennie Morrell, Scott Green, Rod Green & John Bowden, Kay Sterner, Susan Sterner (in memory), Jessica Jenkins, Douglas Thew, Patrick Gilliland, Lee Ann Farruga, Raun Dupuis; old friends Katherine Shapleigh, Kristin McDonald, Michael Moser, Siri Ralph, Russ & Gayle Urban. Also a big thank you to The Tenth Muse Books Publishers and the good folks at Lightning Source for helping get these books into print! Love to all of you!

Table of Contents

Prologue – THE WINTER WIND WHISPERER
1 – FOOTPRINTS IN THE SNOW ~ PAGE 5
2 – A FRIENDSHIP THICKER THAN BLOOD ~ PAGE 23
3 – FIVE FINGER DISCOUNT ~ PAGE 41
4 – THE BLACK OWL RETURNS ~ PAGE 57
5 – REVELATIONS ~ PAGE 69
6 – FOREWARNING ~ PAGE 81
7 – AN OUTCRY OF JUSTICE ~ PAGE 87
8 – THE BIRTH OF A STAR ~ PAGE 101
9 – THE SHIMMER ~ PAGE 111
10 – AWAKENING ~ PAGE 119
11 – THE CALLING ~ PAGE 129
12 – THE RAVEN'S MISTAKE ~ PAGE 135
13 – A FALSE CALM ~ PAGE 143
14 – WITCHBLADE ~ PAGE 153
15 – CIRCLE OF PROTECTION ~ PAGE 161
16 – THE RETURN ~ PAGE 167
17 – THE ANGEL IN THE TREE ~ PAGE 173
18 – A HAUNTING RESEMBLANCE ~ PAGE 177
19 – THE MORNING AFTER ~ PAGE 187
20 – TIME'S SHAKING UP ~ PAGE 197
21 – A CRACK IN TIME ~ PAGE 201
22 – PROPHECY ~ PAGE 209

This book is about peace and stillness.
In the winter, life slows and settles
It rests so that it can be reborn again in the spring

Freya from Wagner's Opera

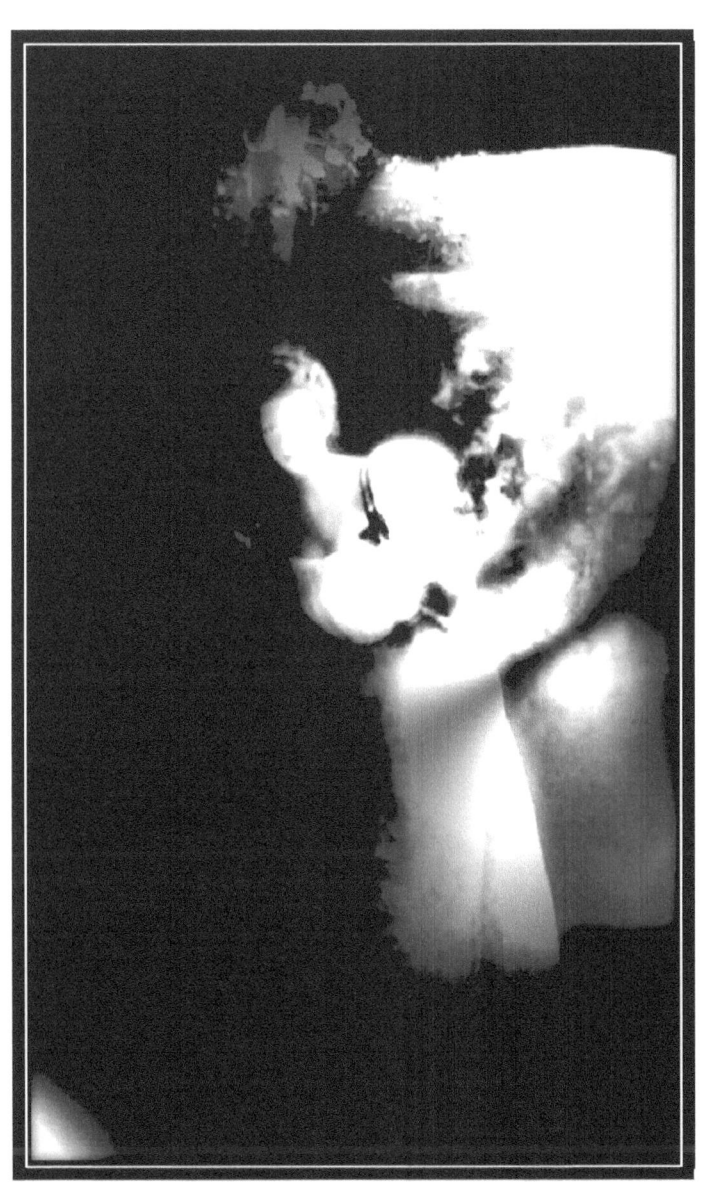

Prologue

THE WINTER WIND WHISPERER

rom out of a deep sleep, I sat up startled by the crackling sound of splintering wood coming from the floorboards of my century old house. A giant hole had opened. A tree grew in my bedroom, and from behind it stepped a skinny, shadow of a pixie or faery. She stood at the foot of my bed staring at me, touched my foot and then returned to the tree. It was dark, but I felt her smile at me. The tree went back into the ground and the floor closed up all around it, leaving me to wonder whether I'd dreamt the whole experience or trust in my heart that what I saw was real.

I turned on the light. At the foot of my bed was a piece of parchment. It appeared to be a letter, not addressed to anyone, but intended for me.

This house harbours a secret book, in a place where time is both found and lost, in the heart and soul, where above and below are conjoined and all things within it are universal. I am here to help you find it. It is a sacred book; one whose energy can be felt from all angles. To open its cover is to call upon me, Rowen, for help. The dryad, who presented you with this letter, is a messenger of mine. I am never seen – not even in shadow, except by those I allow to see – those who have the gift. But you need not see me to know I am here. You will hear my voice. It is scribed here within this letter and so it is within the book. You must find the book for us to move on. It was once considered complete, but there are entire chapters missing – important chapters. Find the missing chapters and return them to the book. Do this by sundown of the winter solstice. I will acknowledge your contribution with a new snowfall by the following sunrise. Mark my words:

if the lost chapters are not found and remain missing, time will not be able to move forward. Those missing chapters are vital keys to your future and ours, for we, the seven sisters of light, must shine through darkness. Now is the time for you to be awakened, little star.

~ Rowen

I couldn't return to sleep after that. *Rowen. Seven sisters of light? Missing chapters?* I rubbed my eyes, attempting to focus on the sleeping cat at the foot of my bed and the puppy that lay on the carpet just beside it. Neither was awake. Peacefully they slept without a care in the world.

I got up out of bed and looked out my bedroom window. Shadow gave a little whimper of curiousity. "Shhh. It's okay, boy. Go back to sleep." My heart wandered to thoughts of Ethan. Was he awake? Just down the unpaved dirt road lived a boy whom I was in love with. All my thoughts were on him tonight.

"I love you, Ethan," I whispered. The window fogged with my breath and then disappeared.

A second glance at the parchment and I slipped it underneath my pillow. Nestling back on my side with my hands tucked neatly under my head, I closed my eyes with hopes of falling asleep; hopes that would manifest themselves as dreams … dreams about a boy who lived at the end of Colby Drive.

Chapter 1

FOOTPRINTS IN THE SNOW

he damp wood of the old, abandoned treehouse made me sneeze. It wasn't an unpleasant smell; perhaps someplace old, with a history of merging generations. The boards and tree legs holding it together looked secure enough, weathered but sturdy. The cold winter wind seeped in through tiny cracks between the windows and the door. It carried with it a haunting whisper. I tried to ignore it. I was with Ethan. Nothing could happen to us.

Evening approached. I had spent the entire day with Ethan. I loved being on winter holidays from school. Christmas was only a handful of days away. I attempted to knit Ethan a scarf, but my knitting skills were anything but what my grandmother could do. Still, I had persisted through it. With any luck, I'd be finished in a few days, just in time to give it to him.

A black, fuzzy blur affectionately and appropriately named Shadow, bounced around my ankles as we both explored the surprisingly well kept treehouse. *Woof.* He bounced with new puppy energy. *Woof.* Ethan showed Shadow a quilted plaid blanket he'd folded up and brought with us. "Come here boy. Lay down. This is your spot." Ethan patted the blanket and Shadow went, rather clumsily, springboarding across the floor, plopped down and sat with tongue drooling outward. *"Pant pant pant, Woof!"* We both laughed.

I peeked out of a large, square window on the east side of the treehouse. "Whoa."

"Yeah. Just don't look down if you get dizzy. It's stable. Do you like it? Built it myself, with some help," he boasted. "Every summer, I'd come back and add something new to it. That's a lot of summers and a lot of chopping wood. It was my Grampa's idea to make it look like a square log cabin."

"I can't believe you built this place! It's so amazing," I began. "I love the smell of wood. It's so earthy, and touching it makes you feel so connected, you know? It's like the wood has a spirit still living inside of it somehow."

"Maybe it does," Ethan smiled as he hung a dream catcher up on a tiny hook on the wall. It had Celtic knots. *An interesting combination.* Ethan was half Irish, half Native. "I thought this place could use a little sprucing up," he said and giggled. "Look at this." He rolled out a slice of tree that was about the size of a skinny bike tire wheel and laid it flat in the center of the room.

My hands felt the bark on the side of the slice. It pulsed. "That must be from a really old tree. Look at all the rings."

"I know. We used it as a makeshift table in our tree fort. Its weathered a lot more since I last saw it."

"You really don't get the same satisfaction at seeing age on other things, like rust on metal, or mold on cheese. Wood kind of takes top marks."

"What about on people? Like wrinkles, those are like tree rings."

"Or lines on your palm."

"There's a whole story written on mine. Makes me wonder who I was in a past life," I said with a naïve laugh. "So, where'd this tree come from? You didn't chop it down did you?"

"No, no, no. It was actually from your property. Gramps had found it a long time ago. He told me that lightning had struck the tree and split it straight in half. Look. You can see the scorch marks."

The haunting whisper returned, chanting an omen. A voice carried on a breeze, whispered through the trees. I listened. The voice seemed to be coming from the tree. I felt compelled to touch the tree; to feel its core.

My hand traced over the center of the tree. Chills ran up my spine. My arm hairs stood on end. I closed my eyes. I felt the electricity still within the tree. It vibrated through me. The tree slice had an electrical charge to it. I pulled my hand away and my arm hairs laid flat again. It was incredible! I didn't know a dead tree could still carry so much energy.

Heavy drafts swept through the wooden room, howling like hungry wolves. Another shiver. The temperature dropped sharply.

Winter came in with a hush. Snow was foreign to me. Most of my life had been spent where the seasons included rain for half the year and laying on the beach for the other half. For the first time, I experienced a cold winter.

I clutched my sweater and pulled the blanket tighter around Ethan and me. "Good thing you built doors on this treehouse. It sounds like a storm is brewing outside. Do you think we'll be okay in here? It's freezing!"

"We'll be fine," he assured. "Come closer."

"Why, Mr. Reilly, you're such a flirt!" I teased in my best southern belle accent.

"Thank you Miss Bell. Who could resist a girl so charming such as yourself?"

We both giggled.

He patted a spot next to him. I snuggled closer, contented with his answer, and his company. He put his arms around me. His presence carried a security I didn't feel on my own. He smelled nice. A little musky, mixed with the scent of the damp wood of the treehouse. I inhaled deeply with my nose pressed into his sweater.

He giggled. "What are you doing?"

"I just want to remember your smell."

"Oh yeah? I'm not going anywhere just yet."

My smile led to a kiss. There were strange noises outside of the treehouse adding to the ambiance. It had started to rain tiny ice pellets that crashed vigorously against the wooden walls. It sounded like we were inside a popcorn popper.

Ethan sat up and went to one of the wooden windows and pulled aside the protective board revealing a screen. He looked out as the ice pellets bounced off the screen in front of his face.

"Wow. Look at it."

I got up and went to the window and looked outside.

"We're going to have to stay here until it lets up," Ethan began. "I don't think we should walk back in this. It's freezing rain really hard.

I haven't seen it like this in several years. It doesn't do this that often in Baltimore."

I clutched my sweater around me and watched my breath as it left my lips when I exhaled. "Close the window please, Ethan. It's really getting cold."

"Sorry to tell you this, but it *is* closed. Here. Crawl inside of this."

I looked at Ethan strangely. The dark green sleeping bag had been propped up against the side of the wall of the treehouse. I wasn't sure what else had crawled inside it before me. "Umm… I'm afraid of bugs, and spiders." Spiders really were in a league all their own.

Ethan giggled a little and nudged me. "Come on. I brought this here yesterday. I thought it might be fun to stargaze here sometime. It's clean of bugs. Promise. See, I'll go inside first." He unzipped the sleeping bag and wiggled inside and patted the side of it. "Come on. I won't bite."

I couldn't resist the invitation, although a sleeping bag was just an outdoor bed and I wasn't sure I felt ready enough to even be in Ethan's bed, let alone his sleeping bag.

"I promise I won't try anything. It's just to keep you warm."

I nuzzled next to him and he zipped us up. The sound of the zipper reminded me that I was in bed with Ethan. I was nervously uncomfortable. Ethan planned this? Was this for more than just stargazing? *Does Ethan want to sleep with me?* My heart raced. Ethan grabbed the blanket and wrapped us both tightly inside. His body heat warmed me.

"Thanks."

"You're welcome." He put his arm underneath my head and let me use it as a pillow.

"You always have a solution, don't you?"

"Hmm?" His eyebrow peeked up into an arch.

"I mean, every time we go somewhere, you know how to get us out of trouble."

"Well I was an eagle scout."

I laughed. There was a pause between us. Ethan brushed a hair off my forehead. The heat within our sleeping bag radiated all the way down to my toes. "Do they give out badges for best kisser?"

He smiled tenderly, but with passion in his eyes. "No, I don't think we had to do that one."

"Too bad. I'd help you practice," I flirted.

"Well, I am a little rusty. It's been almost five minutes since I kissed you last."

"Oh? Five minutes? You're counting?"

"That's five minutes too many," he flirted.

He leaned into me. His breath passed over my lips, but he did not kiss me. He teased with tiny nudges and nuzzles with the side of his nose against mine and trailing the tip of his nose softly against my cheek and to my neck, as though enjoying the smell of me. Having him this close, I already became lost into him. The anticipation of our kiss made my head all fuzzy and floaty, as my breathing was irregular. My heart raced. Time appeared to stop or moving very slowly, like a slow dance and only we existed. He brushed his lips softly against mine, but still he did not press them into a kiss. He pulled back slowly to look me over. My eyes stared dreamily into his. He was hot. I sensed the moment beyond would set me ablaze.

I bit my lower lip. His gaze caught it. Before I could take in my next breath, he lunged and his lips met mine. My hands pressed the sides of his face and held him close. His hand scooped behind my neck. It was only a moment, but a moment so intense it couldn't be duplicated by any other. Not even Sadie would interrupt us.

We kissed. We kissed hard and with such passion that I didn't even notice the ice pellets hitting against the walls of the treehouse. The sound faded and became rhythmic, like drumming, only fueling our kiss instead of inhibiting it. The intensity of our kiss made me uncomfortable and I stopped him. He looked into my eyes. Wildfire ran through them.

"I want you Alyson. I want to be with you."

"Ethan – I – I…"

He kissed me again, and moved his position over me. His kisses moved down to my neck. I felt the blood pulse through it. His kiss, wet and sloppy, inching his way lower. The heat of his breathe melted me into a drippy puddle of desire. It was too intense. Shivers jolted through my core. I kissed his neck back, just below his ear. He'd put cologne there and I inhaled it deeply as my kiss devoured him. His sweat was salty, but not unpleasant. I craved more. Passion overwhelmed us – it turned to lust, something very unbridled, carnal and raw. My clothes itched against my skin and I tugged at them to come off, but knew better. For now, they were the only barrier I had that could keep me from going all the way with Ethan. My desires overran my self control. I wanted to stop him, but didn't want to disappoint either, but I wasn't ready. I wanted him too, but the thought of him inside of me scared the hell out of me. My heart pounded. I pushed lightly against his chest so he'd back off gently. His lips parted from mine and he opened his eyes to catch mine looking back into his sympathetically. He leaned down to kiss me again. I pressed my hand against his chest once again.

"Ethan, stop," I whispered.

"We're just kissing, Alyson." Ethan's eyes eagerly had glanced lower to my sweater.

"I know. But, what comes after? Ethan, I'm scared. I'm not ready to go past the kissing part."

Ethan went silent. I felt his toes through his socks wiggle a little against mine in the bottom of the sleeping bag. He wasn't aware he had done so. He seemed to be analyzing the possibility of not advancing further in our relationship. I looked at him and considered the possibility that two years in age *does* make a difference.

I wasn't ready, but Ethan was.

I suddenly worried that if we didn't take it a step further, I may lose him. Would he go after girls his own age? Girls like Carly? Seniors. *Well I'm almost a junior. Seventeen.*

"I suppose we can maybe ... play ... just a little."

Ethan's eyes lit up like any hormonal teenage boys would have. But mine didn't. I honestly wasn't ready to move forward. I had only recently discovered the kissing part. Why wasn't that enough for Ethan?

I assumed I'd just lay there while he groped his way awkwardly for my bra, but he didn't. He didn't even put a hand on me. I looked at him quizzically.

"Maybe it's okay if you're not ready. I can't help but be eager, Alyson."

"I want to wait."

Ethan's eyes had *how long* written all over them.

"I want to wait until after high school," I said.

"Well that's the end of this year for me."

Both of us fell silent. His comment stung.

"But I'll wait for you," he added and kissed my cheek.

I lit up. "Really?"

"Really. I have my whole life ahead of me too Alyson. I wouldn't want to jeopardize yours with … well … anything you're not ready for."

I smiled.

"Come on. Lay with me for awhile. No pressure. Just lay here with me, and I'll keep you warm," Ethan said. I let out a sigh, feeling slightly defeated by my abstinence and nuzzled into his protective arms.

We laid in silence for several minutes staring up at the ceiling of the treehouse and listening to the sound of rain turning to ice. It wasn't as intense anymore – the storm and with Ethan. The moment had passed. The silence was awkward. I desperately wanted him to say something. I closed my eyes and wondered if Ethan was sincere. *Would he really wait?*

"I know what you're feeling," Ethan said.

"You do?" I smiled when I heard his voice speak.

"Yeah. Sex. It gets in the way."

"Yeah. It seems like everyone else is doing it, so we have to."

"Not really. I haven't jumped off any bridges. And I won't pull you off any either." He rolled onto his side and faced me. "Alyson, I promise you I can wait. I'm content to just be with you."

I really wanted to believe him. *Is there really a rare breed of chivalrous male left? Is Ethan sincere?*

The freezing rain had let up.

I waited for Ethan to unzip the sleeping bag. He didn't.

"Don't you want to head back?" I asked.

"And leave your warmth? I'm not crazy, Alyson. Besides, I told you. I'm content just being with you." He kissed my forehead.

Really? I wondered naively. I had trouble believing him. Images of Carly kept popping into my head. Carly long legs. She was like a new breed of black widow, a seductive spider, crawling into my head and into my sleeping bag with Ethan. I believed I could trust Ethan, but there were senior girls out there who were ready to go beyond kissing. Girl's like Carly. Long-legged Carly, Ethan's friend from a time before he knew me, from a time when she was the one Ethan was content to be with. Carly's body language had said so when she leaned in to give Ethan a kiss on the cheek that day in the parking lot. Ethan giggled. He enjoyed it. Could I trust him? Would Carly seduce him? Or worse, would he seduce her in a moment of unchecked passion?

Shadow circled the bottom of the sleeping bag and found a spot to lie down.

"You know, it'll be hard to teach Shadow to climb trees. This is probably the first time I've carried a puppy up to the treehouse before. Maybe I should build a slide, for when he's older. It's pretty high off the ground you know. At least ten rungs – that's ten feet. It helps to count backwards when coming down."

I looked down to Shadow at the foot of the blankets and then back to Ethan. I listened to what Ethan really said. I should trust him. He'd never broken my trust, so why this awkward doubt? Had my own jealousy of Carly put thoughts into my head? Or was I just protecting my heart from the inevitable heartbreak I'd witnessed my friends go through?

Ethan unzipped the bag and slid out. I felt his warmth go with him as he exited. "I just want to check outside for a moment." He slid back the board revealing the screen. "Whoa. Come look at this."

I got out and went to the window. I looked down to the playground. Every inch of rusted metal was covered in ice. The swings looked like frozen popsicles suspended in time. Thick, long icicles dangled like daggers overhead.

"How are we going to get down?"

Shadow moaned and paced nervous circles around Ethan. Shadow seemed more than his usual impatient puppy self. He was worried.

"It's okay boy," I whispered calmly and bent down to pet the top of the dog's head. Shadow's tail wagged, but remained stiff with concern.

"Very carefully," Ethan noted.

"But Shadow – he might slip."

"I'll wrap him up in a blanket. He won't fall. I promise."

Ethan made a lot of promises to me. He kept them all. The blast of cold air as he opened the door to the treehouse made me gasp as I attempted to catch my breath. "But Ethan, look at all of the ice!"

"I'll be okay. We need to get back before it gets worse."

I trusted him. With Shadow tucked gently in a blanket cocoon underneath Ethan's protective wing, he stepped carefully down the rungs of the ladder. I counted each rung as Ethan descended. ten – nine – eight, and so forth until he reached one. I let out a sigh of relief when he reached the ground. He placed Shadow down and then held open his arms for me to come down.

"I'll catch you if you fall. I promise."

Promises. I laughed a little as I stepped onto the edge of the rung. It was sheathed in ice. I'd never seen ice like that before. I wasn't as focused on descending the ladder as I was on the familiar sight I caught out of the corner of my eye. A large black bird flew towards in my direction. Whether it was Hremm Nevar was irrelevant. I put my foot on the top rung and began to count. ten – nine – eight - … there was no seven. I'd already reached beyond the bottom rung. I'd lost my footing and fallen. Ethan caught me, as promised, but the force of my fall sent us both to the ground.

I looked at him with amazement. "I can't believe you caught me."

"I can't move," Ethan groaned attempting to lift his legs.

"What?"

"I can't move," Ethan repeated. "I can't move my leg."

I looked at Ethan's leg. It bent in a direction it wasn't supposed to. "Oh God," I said. Shadow whimpered anxiously.

"Alyson, you're going to have to go get help. I can't walk back."

"I can't leave you here."

"You have to." Ethan looked to his side. There was blood on the ground. He'd landed on a broken piece of metal.

"Oh my God!" I panicked. "Ethan! You're bleeding!"

"I'll be okay. I can stop the blood. But you have to go!"

Something hard hit me on the top of my head. An ice pellet. The freezing rain had returned. "Why now?" I yelled to God or anyone in the universe who could hear me and would listen. I threw my hands up in frustration.

I ran back to the rungs of the treehouse, dodging ice pellets.

"What are you doing?"

"Getting you a blanket," I yelled to him while getting pummeled by ice pellets.

"NO! GO! Go get Grams! Go get help. I'll be okay, just go!"

But I didn't want to go. I sensed Ethan was in far more trouble than he let on. I began to cry softly. "Ethan." I could barely say his name. "I'll be quick."

"I'll be waiting," he said with an optimistic giggle. He smiled. I looked at his smile. Shadow would stay with him.

"It'll be okay," I tried to convince myself.

I knew the smile hid a large amount of pain behind it.

I took one last look before heading off into the forest. Shadow pranced up behind me. I looked down at him and back to Ethan. His little tail wagged in the snow making a doggy tail snow angel. He groaned every time an ice pellet would make its way to bonk him on the head.

"Go Shadow. Go back to Ethan," I commanded. Shadow halted in place and then ran back to Ethan's side and sat.

"Good boy. Stay there. Stay."

My voice wavered and I held back tears. I knew I had to hurry.

Reluctantly, I ran in the direction of Grams' house. At least I thought I did. The freezing rain made everything difficult to see through.

"Ethan. I have to help Ethan! Why can't I find Grams' house?! Where am I?" Frustrated, I stopped and looked around. I was in the middle of a forest. Every tree looked exactly the same and from where I stood, I didn't know where Colby Drive was. I only knew the path back to the playground. I looked back at my tracks in the frozen ground. The trees broke some of the ice pellets from falling on me, but not all of them. It still felt as if tiny faery sized war planes dropped grenades on me. I felt several welts begin to form into bruises from some of the harder pellets. I looked in front of me. There was only untrodden snow, and now covered in a glossy sheen of ice. We hadn't come this way. *Where is Grams' house?* I was lost. Ethan couldn't walk and needed help, and I was lost. I looked in all directions as my tears froze on my cheeks.

"HELP! Please send me help!" I cried out. Being in the magical world, I looked for a beam of white light or listened for an owl's hoot. Nothing. Nothing that is, until I heard a tiny little "*Woof*" from behind me. I turned around and looked down.

"Shadow!"

Shadow bounced up and down with puppy exuberance. Shadow also bounced like he knew the way to Grams. I decided to follow him. He bounced through the snow; continually looking back to make sure I followed. We came to a clearing in the trees. I looked down to the snow and saw Ethan's footprints from his shoes, perfectly outlined in the ice and snow. I placed my foot inside the shell of this footprint in the snow. His feet cradled mine with every step towards Grams house. This was the way. I followed it until the forest opened up and the dim lights of the houses along Colby Drive shined speckled through the freezing rain. I ran as fast as I could towards Grams house and burst open the door. The house smelled of Christmas.

"Grams!" I yelled throughout the house.

"What is it, Dear?" she approached with oven mitts on her hands. The house smelled of freshly baked pumpkin pie. Shadow bounced up and down at her feet, and barking ferocious puppy barks.

"Ethan's hurt. He needs help. He can't walk." My sentences were short to compensate for the lack of breath I had from running. "And he's bleeding."

"Where is he?" Grams slipped off an oven mitt and reached for the phone, her voice quivering and hands shaking gently. Her feeble wrinkled fingers dialed 9-1-1 as I spoke. "I'm too old to go trekking into the forest in this weather. When help comes, you'll have to lead them to him Alyson."

"I know. I will." I had Shadow to help find the path for me.

Tears streamed down my face. I thought of Ethan, sitting alone in the middle of a frozen playground. I wondered if he was cold, or if it hurt to be bleeding. *He bled because of me. He bled because he promised to catch me and I wasn't paying attention. It was my fault he was hurt.*

I looked down to pet Shadow and scratch his head, but Shadow was not there. Shadow was gone. He had bolted out the door in the direction we'd just come from. A lonely raven sat perched atop one of the frozen trees in Grams yard. Its presence bothered me.

"Shadow" I yelled.

I started to run after him. "You can't go. You need to wait for the help to arrive. They're on their way, Alyson. They're on their way. Ethan's going to be fine. He's got angels watching over him." Grams hugged me.

It was difficult to swallow. Worried tears continued to find their way down my cheeks. I'd hoped that Shadow found his way back to Ethan. I worried I wouldn't remember.

Abigail, help.

The paramedics showed up and Grams greeted them in the doorway.

"It's my grandson. Alyson can take you to him." She put one hand behind my shoulder and led me to the door. "Take them to him, Alyson." Grams looked at me oddly. "Here, take this. It belonged to Ethan's father."

In my hand, she placed a compass.

How did Grams' know I didn't remember? I wondered.

"Thanks. It's this way," I led them confidently in the direction of the playground. I pulled back several icy branches which framed the opening mouth of the clearing where the playground was. We made our way into to the clearing and to the playground. Ethan sat on the ground, but had slid closer to underneath a tree. There was a large blood trail on the snow. Next to his side sat Shadow.

"Ethan, I'm back and I brought help. Ethan? Ethan?!"

I ran to him and knelt by his side.

Ethan wasn't moving.

"Ethan!" I yelled.

"We've got an emergency here," one of the paramedics yelled into his radio and another one held me back. They talked and moved very fast as the rest of the world appeared to move in slow motion.

"Puncture wound. Rusty bike. Looks like he fell directly back on a pedal, or one of these broken wheel spokes. Might've hit an organ. Get a stretcher. Splint the leg."

I held back intense gasps. "Ethan?" I whispered through tears.

"Stay back, miss. We'll take it from here." The authoritative shout of his words made an invisible boundary between me and Ethan. I could not pass it.

Shadow ran over to me and moaned at my feet. I scooped his little puppy body into my arms. Something smeared over my hand. It was wet and dark. Shadow was covered in Ethan's blood. He jumped up to lick my frozen cheeks.

I was rattled. I couldn't stop shaking. I held the blood covered puppy cradled in my arms. He whimpered. Waterfalls of tears washed down my face like rain, but my voice couldn't speak intelligible words. Shadow's eyes mirrored my own. I whimpered.

"Ethan. Please don't die."

Chapter 2

A FRIENDSHIP THICKER THAN BLOOD

he sirens echoed inside the ambulance, shattering my eardrums. "That's quite a bruise you have on your cheek. You and your boyfriend get into a fight?" one of the paramedics asked me.

"What? Umm... no, nothing like that." I put my hand to my cheek and felt it. It was frostbitten. "It's probably just from the ice."

"Let's have a look when we get there."

I didn't care about me. I cared about Ethan. I looked at him. He wasn't conscious. My mind raced to the moments of us before in the treehouse; him looking down on top of me, kissing me. To see him before me unconscious and barely breathing was surreal. His eyes were closed. I wanted him to open them. Shock set in.

"What's going to happen to him?"

"Well, the emergency room doctors will take a look at your friend and –"

"I know that already. I mean, is he going to die?" I said with such a sullen voice I began to cry. I'd never felt this way before.

There was a long pause. A pause that assured me it was a possibility.

Ethan can't die. He's only eighteen! He's my Prince Charming. In what fairy tale book did the Prince die first? And leave his fair maiden to slay the dragon herself?

At the hospital, the back doors of the ambulance swung open and Ethan was rushed on a stretcher into the big sliding doors of the ER.

Grams hugged me as we waited together in the waiting room. "I called Josie." It took a moment to register. "She's going to catch the next flight back from Paris."

I'd finally get to meet Ethan's mom. I knew if Grams' called her that it was probably serious. I felt like I wanted to throw up.

"Grams. Is Ethan going to be okay?"

She didn't say anything immediately. Instead she took out a handkerchief and wetted it and brought it to my face. As she wiped it, I saw it covered with blood. Ethan's blood. I looked at the concern hiding behind Grams' eyes.

"I hope so, dear. But there's a possibility we both could lose him." Her voice was soft spoken and shaky. "I barely remember Harding, my brother, when he passed away. Death seems to have no preference for age. He was very close to Ethan's age. I pray we don't lose him, dear."

This couldn't be happening. ... But it was.

Time trudged slowly on. The doors opened and the doctor approached us. I watched his feet peek out from underneath the blue pastel scrubs. Every footstep he took made my heart skip a beat. He stopped before us and opened his mouth to speak. My eyes gazed forward. *Was he or wasn't he?* Time had frozen. I ceased to blink. I waited in fear for him to tell us Ethan was dead.

"We are looking for a match. He needs a blood donor. He has a rare blood type. Are either of you compatible?"

Without thinking I blurted out, "I'll do it." I wanted to crumble to the floor. There was still hope.

"Well chances of you being the same blood type or a match are rare, but if you're willing, we can test you. Come with me."

He looked to Grams. "You need to hold onto your blood, Miss." He smiled and winked at her. "I'll let you know if she's a match. In the interim, please contact other available kin."

My mom and dad rushed into the ER.

"Would somebody please tell me what's going on here?" Dad asked around. Grams greeted him.

The doors closed behind me. I followed the doctor around a few twists and turns into a long corridor. He pushed open another big door. Mom came running through to find me.

"Grams told me. Are you sure you are okay to do this?" Mom asked as we walked.

"I'm fine. I'm more worried about Ethan than a little needle prick." I tried not to sound nervous.

The procedure felt like it took several hours, although it probably wasn't that long. Miraculously, I was a match for Ethan's blood type. Ethan now had a pint of my blood flowing through him.

I sat with Grams in the waiting room. I stared endlessly at the vending machine. My stomach grumbled. A nurse brought me some orange juice.

"Any news?" Dad asked.

"Still waiting." We waited for what felt like eternity. Ethan had gone into surgery. A doctor emerged and we all sat up in our chairs. My Dad stood and I held Grams' hand.

"He is stable."

There was a heavy sigh let out from each of us in the waiting room. The doctor continued. "He will need to be watched for signs of tetanus, and he's lost a lot of blood. I'm sure he would like to see you."

I went to Ethan's bed and knelt beside him. He could barely open his eyes.

"Crawl in," he joked. "There's room."

I threw myself over him and hugged him. Tears left my eyes and dripped onto him.

"Hey, you're getting me all wet here."

"Sorry." I wiped tears off my cheeks and giggled. "I'm just really happy to see you!"

"I'm happy to see you too. Guess everyone thought I was a goner."

"Yeah well. You're one hell of an actor, but certainly not ready to take your final bow. You really scared me. Don't do that again."

"Well stop falling out of tree houses, silly."

I grabbed a nearby pillow from the adjacent orange lounge chair and mocked throwing it at him.

"Hey now. Take it easy." I set the pillow down. "Come closer," he said gently.

I leaned down to him.

"Thanks for being there when I needed you," he whispered and kissed my cheek.

Grams knocked on the door. "May I interrupt?" she asked.

"It's okay. I'll leave." I started to sweep up my coat into my arms when Gram insisted I stay. I put my coat back down in the orange chair and sat down.

Grams hugged Ethan. "You put a scar into me. But my grandson is tough as nails. I had faith you'd pull through. Your father wouldn't let you join him just yet, Ethan. It's not your time to leave. This family has already been shaken enough. Now I've been around for a long time, and I've seen a lot of things in my days, but to witness what I witnessed today was reminiscent of the day we all lost Harding, my brother."

Ethan and I listened attentively.

"So many people loved him. It was a tragedy, one of the worst kind. He was just one year shy of his eighteenth birthday that day his horse bolted him into a fence. That kind of shock isn't easily forgotten and is easily remembered when emotions such as this get stirred up. I remember how difficult it was for those two sisters to handle Harding's death. Let's see, Elsbeth. No, that's not it. Emelia. Emelia Finch and her sister Sadie. Yes, those were the girls. Oh how Emelia loved him. She would come by daily to visit with Harding and likewise, he would visit her. They had so much in common. You might even have jested that they shared a brain," Grams said with a smile. "You see, for Harding, Emelia was like his lighthouse. She helped him get through the storms and safely to harbor. And he was there for her, to escape the rocky waters at home and drift out to sea with him. They complimented each other. It is a rare kind of love. I hope you both know where I'm going with all of this."

Ethan nodded.

"Just take care to love each other, and if it's meant to be, you always will."

I looked at Ethan, but also saw Harding in him. They did look identical, save for being three fourths of a century apart in age. I thought of the turmoil Emelia had to endure when she witnessed his death, and the aftermath of Sadie and her curse.

"Thanks Grams," Ethan said and pulled her down to give her a kiss on the cheek.

Grams smiled warmly at him. "I'll be going now. I'm relieved to hear the news."

I wasn't prepared for what followed. In walked a bouquet of balloons suspended on long strings and held by hands and a pair of long legs. The balloons parted and a girl's voice said, "Heya cutie. Heard you were in the hospital. My brother's a nurse here." The voice behind the balloons belonged to Carly.

"Oh heya, Care Bear."

Care Bear?

I let out a pseudo giggle and waved. "Hi."

She tied the balloons to the metal bar at the headboard of his hospital bed.

"Those ought to cheer you up."

"Thanks." Ethan looked pleased that Carly had visited him in bed. I tried not to get jealous. After all, they were just friends. Just really close friends ... with a lot of history between them.

"I can't stay. Matt's taking me to see *Santa's Revenge* or something like that."

Ethan laughed. He looked at me. I forced a laugh too.

"Mm'k. Well thanks for coming by. Thanks for the balloons."

"Welcome," she bubbled. She waved. "Bye Alyson."

She remembers my name?

"Bye." I waved back.

"She's nice. She's going to try to get into the same college as me in the Fall."

"Oh?"

"Yeah. It'll be nice to see a familiar face every day."

"Umm... yeah."

My soul sulked.

I still had close to a year and a half until I could begin to think about colleges.

"Umm... which colleges are you looking at?" I innocently asked, hoping his answers were local, or at least in the same city.

"Well, I'm thinking of a few places. VA Tech is one."

"That's so far away."

Ethan heard the upset in my voice.

"Hey. I know it's a little far away. Just a couple of hours by bus. But you can visit me and I can come see you. We won't be that far apart. And besides, we still have at least until next fall before we have to think about it. Let's take it one day at a time, okay? I barely just survived making it to graduation," he added with a smile.

I nodded. I spent a while at Ethan's side, lying next to him in the hospital bed. We both fell asleep.

Ethan?

Hmm?

Are you dreaming?

Yeah, I think so.

There was a long pause.

Alyson?

Yeah?

Are you dreaming?

Yeah.

Oh.

Hippopotamus.

I sat up. Ethan sat up and looked at me with an odd expression. "Did you just … did we just share a dream?"

"You felt that too?"

"Yeah?"

"That was really weird," he said, freaked.

I wondered if Ethan's blood transfusion from me had linked us.

"Why did you say hippopotamus?" Ethan asked.

"You *did* hear me!" I paused to reflect. "I'm not sure. I think I wondered if you really were sharing a dream with me, and I figured you'd remember that."

Footsteps approached and quiet nurses' chatter filled the air just outside the door. I quickly evacuated Ethan's bed and scooted into a nearby chair. A nurse walked in and approached Ethan's bedside.

"Doing any better?" she asked, setting down a cup of water for him.

Ethan looked for the pills. She didn't have any.

"You should drink the water. It has healing qualities."

Ethan took the cup and drank from it.

"See. You don't need the pain pills anymore. I pray you heal quickly. I know you will."

She smiled and walked away, leaving the room.

"Was that your regular nurse?" I asked Ethan. "I thought your nurse was a guy?"

"That wasn't my regular nurse."

Ethan peeled back the white hospital sheet covering him. His leg had a thick piece of gauze bandage covering his wound. It was covered in blood.

"I can change that for you," I told him. The nurse had left behind several self-adhesive gauze pads for him to change as necessary.

Ethan rolled softly to the side, revealing a cheek. I blushed.

He blushed too.

"It's okay. I appreciate the help."

I smiled and scraped the tip of my nail against the corner of the adhesive square on Ethan's upper thigh. I expected him to wince as I peeled back the corner, taking several leg hairs with it.

"It'll be easier if I do it like a Band-Aid," I said, ripping the square back quickly. Ethan let out a small yelp. "Oh don't be such a baby," I teased him as I peeled open the new bandage and prepped it for his leg. I turned back to the wound and fell silent.

I stared at the square outlined on his leg. The gauze I'd just tossed in the garbage was bloody. I'd seen the wound. His leg had been punctured. I reached to his leg and stroked my fingers along the stitches. They fell off to the ground. There was no wound.

I was speechless.

"I'm not a baby," Ethan playfully put up his defenses and caught a look of my eyes looking at his leg. "What? What is it? Did it get worse?"

I was slow to respond. "No. No, it didn't get worse. It – it got better." I stuttered as my eyes stared in disbelief. It was a miracle!

Ethan put his hand to his thigh and pried his eyes to scan his buttocks and upper thigh area. He slid his hand over his leg in shock. "Huh? How?"

His regular nurse opened the door. "And how's my favourite patient doing?" he said politely as he set a cup of water down on the tray, alongside a tiny paper cup of pain pills. He looked curiously to the other cup. He peeked at Ethan's chart quickly. "Has another nurse checked on you? Have you already had your pain pills?"

Ethan, still in shock, looked to his leg and showed the nurse. Before long, Ethan had a roomful of nurses and doctors checking on him. He was now a phenomenon.

"But how did he heal so quickly? I've never seen blot clot that fast, let alone a seven inch gash totally disappear in the course of hours. That isn't possible," one doctor shouted.

"Well he healed somehow. We're not all hallucinating are we? Just look with your own eyes."

I watched them bicker as they ushered me out of the room. I protested, but finally got shoved in the hallway with the door slammed in my face.

"Look at them scurry," a voice said standing next to me. "Look at them scurry and try to play God. They can't accept a miracle when they see one. Maybe they should look with their eyes closed and their minds and hearts open. They should learn to trussssst."

I looked at the woman. It was the nurse who had come into see Ethan. Looking at her more closely revealed yet another miracle... Her blind silver eyes glimmered at me. *Abigail.*

"I'm happy your friend is safe Alyson. You need to keep watch over him. He has a very important role to play in this thing called life."

"Abigail. How did you –?"

"Sometimes you ask too many questions when really, you should already know the answers. Listen to the voice you can't hear. Listen to your heart."

The door opened and Ethan snuck out. "Thank goodness for curtains. They think I'm in the bathroom. Quick. Let's get out of here."

Abigail smiled.

Ethan looked her in the eyes. "Hey, it's the gypsy lady."

Abigail knew Ethan had recognized her. She snapped her fingers and we were gone.

"Abigail?"

"Yes, Alyson?"

"Why'd you bring us here?" I looked around. We were in the treehouse again.

"Sleep. When you wake, this will all have been a dream." She snapped her fingers and Ethan gently collapsed onto the blanket. "He will be fine. He is healed. Healing the body is easy, the spirit takes much more time – lifetimes you might say."

She stepped out of the treehouse door, and hovered in mid-air as though in flight. "That was a gracious thing you did today to save your friend. He now has a part of you running through his veins. You and he already discovered the link. That link is stronger now. It is both a blessing and a curse, dear." She waved her hand to the dream catcher on the window and made it spin. "Be watchful not to give Ethan your nightmares. He won't be able to handle them."

"Nightmares? I don't have nightmares."

"You will," she warned. "I fear this is an omen of something to come. Something worse than Hremm Nevar."

"What could be worse than Hremm Nevar?"

"The end of the world. Rather, the end of what you currently know and see as belief. The world has lost its spirit. Humankind suffers unnecessarily."

In any other circumstance, I would've laughed at the concept. The world ending. But this was Abigail's words. Abigail never lied. Abigail was as pure as truth would ever be.

"Fear not Alyson," she instructed. "It is not a Death, but a transformation. There will be a new world that follows. Something humankind has waited for, for a long time. But it will be up to them to build it, to find it, for it exists within themselves."

"To build what?"

"It's like this treehouse, Alyson. This treehouse was built out of love. It has spirit. Without the love, it would just be wooden boards. It is not the nails that hold it together, but the spirit of Ethan's father and grandfather, the memories which gives it infallible strength. The treehouse is just a shell, but the true gem lies within. Just as you are just a body covered in flesh, but the true gem exists within… your soul…

your spirit. Fill it with love and you will be able to ascend to heights greater than you've ever imagined. Without love, you will be as hollow and empty as Hremm Nevar himself. Until humankind learns to love, to build it, take care of it, and grow it into the garden of paradise they seek, they will only know how to destroy. Humankind refuses to accept miracles happening around them daily. You only ever watch the bad news on television. War, famine, suicide, murder." She shook her head in sadness. "Do you want me to tell you how I know of this? Do you want me to take you back several hundred years? Thousands even? Pull out your pocketwatch Ethan gave you and look at it."

I didn't have Ethan's pocketwatch with me.

"Yes you do," she confirmed. She had read my thoughts. "Look in your pocket. Where else would you find extra time? In a black hole?" she said with a smirk.

I looked quizzically at her and peeked into the black hole of my empty pocket. I reached inside and pulled out the pocket watch. Amazingly enough, it was there. She silently watched what I would do next. I opened the pocket watch and stared into the shiny gold mirror that reflected back at me.

"Now listen to my voice and only my voice," she began. Her voice was deep and solid, and the monotonous tone lured me into a state of hypnosis. "I will take you back, but it is up to you to find how to return. Bring with you the knowledge from the past, and how you can use it to build a better future. Learn from your mistakes, for in each life, it has been only the body that has deceased. The spirit remains. Your memories remain with it. You will see that I too, am not perfect. In essence, quite the opposite. You will see my former life and in it, hopefully will see your future."

"You say the body can die, but the spirit remains. But wouldn't that make us all ghosts?"

"A ghost has not found the light. A ghost has not returned home to be reborn. It remains Earthbound, where it feels it remains, but it is wrong. We belong to our Creator. If a ghost does not return, it cannot rest. It cannot be reborn. It cannot be healed."

"What about those who are reborn? Can the spirit die?"

"It can die, or be corrupted, even captured – as though held hostage, where shards of you are missing. Without them you cannot be complete. A thief of souls is worse than one who steals blood from your body. A soul vampire is one who steals your spirit. You know of whom I speak."

"Hremm Nevar?"

"Yes."

"If he steals your spirit completely, you will be as he is. He lured Sadie into this trap. She has been rescued, as has your friend Sara. But he still seeks you, as you are still an innocent."

"I shall be careful."

"Just be. The past is written. Learn from it." Abigail's eyes flashed at me. It was time.

I stared into the swirling mirror of the pocket watch. It hypnotically pulled me through time. I closed my eyes and felt the vacuum's compression sucking me through the portal and falling to the ground.

"See, I told you I'd catch you," a man laughed as I landed on top of him on the mattress of a four post bed. I lifted myself off of him and looked at him oddly. This clearly wasn't Ethan. *Where was I? What was that awful smell?* There was something unusual about him, and not just the stench. It wasn't the sweet smell of Ethan's cologne. This was an unbathed man that no doubt even a fly wouldn't come near. Instincts told me to flee, but fear kept me close. "Sweetheart? How's about a kiss?"

His hairstyle was different. It looked old-fashioned. Then I noticed his clothing. He wasn't dressed in anything you would typically find in a present day department store rack. He had on a suede blazer jacket and a shallow-dome crowned, black felt bowler hat, otherwise known as a billycock. His black shoes were dirt covered and scuffed. On the tip of his left shoe, there was a tattered hole that appeared as though he'd shot himself in the foot. He had a pistol in his belt. He lit up a cigar. "There. That's nice. Nothing like a stogie after a hard day of bamboozling and embezzling from the old folks. They didn't even see it coming. Nope. Haha!"

What was this man talking about? Where was I?

He added while sorting through stacks of gold and silver coins. It was dirty money. "Just like Robin Hood. Steal from the poor and make ourselves richer."

"That wasn't Robin Hood," I said defensively. "He stole from the rich and gave to the poor."

"Sweetie pie. Are you going soft? Because if I thought for one moment that you were going to jinx me or sell me out to a nark, it'd be your last breath." He winked at me while tapping his pistol against his hip.

I didn't know who this man was. I looked around as the background settled in around us. I obviously wasn't in the treehouse anymore.

We were in an old, dusty room. Pale yellow smoke-stained wallpaper clung helplessly to the wall. Dark, bulky furniture dominated the room, including a four post bed. He flung his hat and it landed on one of the posts.

"You know I'm kidding, doll face. I'd never harm a hair on your body. It looks too good and it'd be a shame to taint such ... purrrrfection." He smacked his lips and took a long drag on his cigar as he reclined farther back in his easy chair. He looked me up and down with a devilish grin and lust in his eyes. I looked away from him. The smell made me want to wretch.

I walked to the mirror and looked at myself staring back at me. The image before me startled me. I was me, but this wasn't my body. I looked into my eyes in the mirror. They were the same, but the body was different. This *clearly* wasn't the present. I pinched my arm. I wasn't dreaming. I was really here, wherever here was.

Abigail? Oh Abigail, I wish you could hear me. What's going on? I wish I knew what year it was.

I'd stepped into the past. Where I landed, I had yet to find out.

Chapter 3

FIVE FINGER DISCOUNT

y reflection revealed a different me entirely. My hair was piled atop my head with long spiral tendrils falling out of it. It was brown and I wore more makeup on my face than my mom would ever let me play dress up with. I wore a bonnet of black silk velvet with blue, black and white striped ribbon, coq feathers and a festoon of black silk satin loop, which I loosened and removed. My hair spilled from underneath it. I looked down to my chest. It was laced up in a white whale bone corset which matched the white leather ankle boots, similarly laced. Separating the two was a very fluffy tiered skirt. I lifted up my skirt to reveal my leg. Strapped to my thigh was a wavy dagger. I let out a tiny gasp. *I was thieving, parlour girl.*

"Don't tease me," he said taking another drag on his cigar. The smell made me want to gag. I let down my skirt again. *Apparently a very good one.*

Whoever this was in a past life, I didn't want to know him. But my intuition told me I had to. There had to be a lesson in here. Abigail hadn't sent me back in time just for fun.

I felt something inside my corset itching me. I modestly turned away from the man and reached into my bosom. I pulled out not one, but three men's wallets. I also pulled out what appeared to be a satiny blue and gold trimmed marble bag. Peeking inside revealed women's jewelry and gemstones. There must've been at least ten different rings inside! *I'm a thief?*

"Let's see what you've pilfered today my sweets. Come sit on my lap." He let out an obnoxious slap against his knee, puffed again on the cigar and grinned. I didn't like it one bit.

I ran to the door and pulled on the knob. It had been locked. He got up from the bed and pushed me up against the door. "You won't steal from me!" He yanked the wallets from my hand.

"I wasn't stealing. Take them. You can have them," I shouted at him.

He spit on the floor. "How dare you talk back to me!" He raised his hand to slap me. I winced as I felt the sting against my cheek. "Learn your place, woman!" He stormed across the room. I felt up at my cheek and began to cry.

Three hard pounds knocked from the other side of the door. "Hey, let us in, Freddie. We gots a new toy with us."

He pushed me aside from the door and let three men in the room. One of them pointed and laughed at me as they noticed my cheek. "Your woman getting frisky with you again, Freddie? You gotta teach 'em their place. One toe over the line and they'll run your life forever. You gotta show 'em who's in control."

Another one laughed. "Hehe... yeah, control."

I cowardly crept into a corner. This scenario I'd landed in was about to go from bad to worse. Four of them and only one of me. I sized them up individually and felt the cold steel blade of the dagger hiding underneath my skirt. I knew I was only moments away from having to use it. Fear ran through me.

"Hey Freddie. How's about I show your gal a little lovin?" the one with the revolver said as he approached me.

"Go ahead," said the man they called Freddie. "She's forgotten some of her moves though. Might need to jog her memory."

"Don't worry. She'll remember."

As he approached me with lust and danger in his eyes, he penetrated my comfort zone. Something came over me. I was no longer fearful, but empowered. I smiled at him and gave a wink, brushing hair off my shoulder and bending over to reveal hints of mounds of fleshy cleavage no man could resist. I found the ruffled edge of my skirt and lifted it slowly, inching up my thigh, but not letting the dagger in view.

He laughed and bellowed. "Now there's the little tart we all know and love. Show me what you got."

I reached for the dagger. Before I knew it, the hilt stuck out of his chest and the blade buried deep within. The man gasped. I pulled out the dagger but surprise remained buried in his eyes. Before he collapsed to the floor, I'd thieved off two rings and his wallet.

"I'll show you what I've got." I screeched at them and waved the dagger. Each of them had a gun but oddly enough, they feared me. The tip of the dagger pointed at each of them, including the man called Freddie. The men were still in shock as they stared at the body on the floor. The man called Freddie smiled at me. It was an odd smile. Almost one that confirmed he already knew what I had planned. I swiped the wallets and left the hotel room.

They didn't come after me right away. Instead, I heard two gunshots from inside the room. I hid behind a plant. The door opened and the man called Freddie walked out. He kissed the new revolver he'd picked off one of the guys. He winked at me inside the plant. He knew. Somehow though, I knew too. I had the sudden realization that I was his partner in crime. Someone I loved to hate and hated to love. It was obviously a tumultuous relationship.

"You know I'd never do anything to hurt you, don't you?" he reached inside the plant and pulled me out from behind it. How he found me in that clever hiding place, I'll never know.

A man in a sheriff uniform ran up the hallway towards us. The man pulled me in for a kiss and swept me inside the tight elevator. His breath made me want to be sick. The sheriff glanced at us debating whether or not to interrupt what appeared to him as a passionate moment, but spoke anyways. When he looked away, I gave him a look of disgust and hatred for being treated so callously.

"Hey. Did you two hear gunshots?" he yelled at us.

"Yeah, yeah. It came from inside that room over there," Freddie shouted. The sheriff opened the door. "Looks like they had an altercation and shot each other," he concluded and looked back to us. "Good riddance. Them 'Boys' are all the same. That's two of 'em less in the world to have to get rid of. Makes my job easier."

Freddie pressed a lever to get the elevator to go down. The doors closed in front of us just as the sheriff shouted for us to wait. We'd escaped.

We fled out of the swinging wooden double doors of the hotel and into the dust streets.

"This way." He yanked my arm and forced me to run with him. We ran down a dark alley, tripping over several drunks surrounded by glass bottles. "May as well drink it before they ban it," one of them slurred.

Freddie spun me around wildly at the end of the alley. No exit. Just a door. "Down there," he shoved and I almost tripped.

"Hey," I scowled back at him. He glared at me. I cowered and followed him. I felt like his pet dog. But my uncertainty of the times and my means I had to work with left me leaning onto Freddie like a rock. I knew in my heart that I had to get away from him. His energy was so hostile, and I felt like his prisoner, doing his bidding.

Buskers of all types littered the streets. One particularly drunk and dirty man yelled in my direction. "Damn women. You gals think you can run everything. Keep her in her place," he yelled at Freddie. He swigged back on his bottle as a loud belch escaped the bellows of his overfed stomach. Music and gunfire sounded through the alleyway.

I looked to Freddie expecting another slap. Two women passed us in the alley. They both batted their eyelashes at him. Oddly enough, I felt jealous. They giggled and snubbed their noses as they walked by and into the doorway close to us. As they opened the door, the sound of live music grew louder.

"Want to go in?" I suggested, hoping my change in tone would distract him.

"Yeah. I could use a stiff drink and a couple of wenches." He opened the door and I prepared to follow him in. "Wait here," he directed as the door closed in my face.

I couldn't believe it. What was this time? This obviously was someplace in the past, but why was I here? *Couple of wenches?*

I felt a tap on my shoulder. I looked to see Abigail standing nearby, although it wasn't Abigail. It was the gypsy. Her eyes were the same as Abigail's, but that was the only similarity.

"Hey. It's you," I said with recognition. The woman had no idea what I referred to and looked at me concerned.

"Come with me child," she directed. I followed her. "My name is Doña Bella, but most people just call me Madame Belladonna. Come inside." She opened the wooden door to the tavern. "You can work for me now. I run this orphanage of lost souls. We're all friends here."

Inside, I was surrounded by women of dubious virtue, whom, despite their class, displayed perfect drawing-room manners. Overhearing their conversations revealed a certain competition of success in picking pockets, shoplifting and "ways with the gentlemen." I glanced to a low lit corner to see Freddie nuzzling with the two girls that passed us outside. He was surrounded by several dark bottles and shot glasses.

Belladonna ushered me to a different area of the tavern. As I approached, I saw an eyeful of scantily clad women all seducing gentlemen travelers and other way-ward souls. One looked up from a passionate kiss at Belladonna as she pulled the beads aside and revealed a lounge, similar to the inside of her gypsy caravan. "Back here, through the beads."

Lush carpets and tapestries lined the floors and walls. The scents of heavy perfume mixed with tobacco and incense lingered thick enough to taste. Probably a good thing considering the condition of the gentlemen the women had to seduce. *Disgusting! Pigs are cleaner than that!*

There were thick doors just beyond the edges of the room in the tavern, leading to a hallway of rooms for more private affairs. A gentleman scattered some coins on the table to pay for the booze and was led off to one of these rooms by an obviously experienced woman.

"So you won't be working for Freddie anymore, got it? You'll be working for me," Belladonna directed.

I wanted to ask her just *what* I would be doing. Thieving? Pickpocketing? Just how did I obtain all those wallets and rings anyways?

I caught glimpse of a newspaper:

1887? I paused to reflect. I had traveled through time. *Question is, why am I recognizing everyone's soul when their outer appearance looks so different? Is this some sort of gift? I was able to see Abigail as the gypsy back at the RenFest, and here she stands before me, only now I am in her time! What am I doing here?*

"Belladonna?"

"Please just call me Bella. Why be so formal? We're all friends here. Come in, come in. Don't stand in the doorway. It's bad luck." She waved her hands in a welcoming gesture. I stepped inside the room in the back.

A very familiar face greeted me. "Aye, 'tis Wendy. Pleasure to meet ya. Care for a drink lassie? Perhaps to see a few tricks?"

I stumbled upon the very thought. How old was I anyways? I had to find a mirror. Conveniently, there was one on the adjacent wall. I looked at myself. I was disheveled. My hair was mopped upon my head, and sat uncomfortably like a bird's nest on a wobbly branch. I let it down and it cascaded down my back. My eyes peered down. Things certainly had changed since the present day. I had much more cleavage. I could easily have been mistaken for one of these bar maids. *And I'm plump!? Well, curvy. I look healthy at least.*

I turned around to take a step backwards and fell across a barstool, sending me tumbling quite wobbly across the bar and spilling myself across a peanut shell strewn floor. I stood up and picked the shells out of my hair and brushed off my dress as though nothing had happened.

"Miss?" she repeated.

"Oh sorry," I stumbled on my words this time. "Yes. I'll take whatever is, umm, on the house."

She smiled. "A little short for change me lassie? Come see me Wendy and I can teach ye a trick or two." She came over to me and judged me, looking me up and down. "Yep. Plump in all the right places. Everywhere!" she giggled. "That's how me boys like us. 'Specially me Duncan."

She slapped something brown in a glass in front of me that appeared to have grown soap scum along the top of it. The glass was chipped in several places and was slowly leaking out the beverage.

"Thanks," I said. I took a sip and chewed it. "Mmm," I faked through a smile.

"Oops, I gave ye the wrong glass. That's the fat from me bacon grease."

It took all I could do not to throw up. Whatever she handed me tasted like fire, but I washed it down anyways. It cleared the taste of the fat, but only by burning off all of my taste buds.

There appeared to be two of her standing at the bar.

"Whoa Nelly. Haven't ye ever drank before? That was 100 year old malt whiskey. Sweet, wasn't it?" she teased. "The only thing stronger would be me pappy's moonshine!"

A gentleman walked in through the beads. Wendy quickly tucked a pink rosebud in my bosom. Apparently the colour meant I was more innocent. I would cost extra. Something about *deflowering the maidens*.... I didn't want to know.

"Well don't just stand there lassie, go saddle him. Stallions don't ride through these parts too often."

I wasn't sure what she meant. He did appear to be a catch. The eyes of every woman in the bar were on him, but his were on me. He sat down and leaned forward on the counter.

"Buy the lady here a drink, on me. Best of the house."

Feeling very tipsy, I smiled at him. Wendy gave me a nudge with her hip, almost knocking me over on top of him. "Oops, me Wendy is a bit clumsy when she's drunk." She lowered down to pick up a handkerchief, her bosom on full display. The gentleman's eyes were not only diverted, but she grabbed the crook of his elbow and led him away.

Belladonna approached me. "Take out the rose. You're not ready. I don't want to lose any customers and Joe is one of my highest paying. He treats the girls with respect. You should be so lucky to find a man like that. Just like a horse, we have to break you in. You can leave at any time if you're not going to do business."

Belladonna was beautiful. She wore a bustier that left her midriff bare, and a gypsy skirt flowed from her hips. Her obvious talent was belly dancing. She moved in a way I'd seen snakes move. On her hips were round discs and coins. Light from the candles bounced off them as she moved. Very mysterious and taking interest in me more so than I knew why. "Are you ready or shall I show you the door?"

As she spoke, in walked another man. It was Seamus. I approached and she held my arm back. "No. This one is mine. He doesn't visit often enough."

"Oh, he's high paying is he?" I tried to fit in and get along.

"No. This one is special. I love him. He's never been—a customer, if you understand me."

I thought of Ethan. I knew exactly what she meant.

Belladonna approached Seamus, not seducing him by dancing, but instead rushing to be at his side. He presented her with an exotic and delicate lily and kissed the top of her hand. "Seamus, I told you not to come in here. You'll be seen," she warned him as she ushered him just out of view, but not out of earshot for me to overhear them.

"I had to see you Bella. I have a surprise for you."

Belladonna gave him a look of *you shouldn't have*.

"Come on. I tied her up outside."

Knowing where we were upturned my eyebrow. My curiousity was more than piqued. I watched them go outside and then snuck behind them. Seamus took Belladonna's hand and put it the reins of a horse. She was a gorgeous beige coloured horse with a wild and long mane. She was branded with two hearts intertwined on her hip.

"I'd like you to meet – Gypsy Epona. She's one of the finest of her breed. She can help you pull your caravan so you can leave this place."

"Seamus – I – I can't. You know I can't leave."

"Sure you can." He grabbed both of her hands and held them inside of his own. "Come away with me. Let that beggar wench Wendy run the place. We both know she belongs amongst the thieves and other shifty-eyed scoundrels and tramps that walk through those tavern doors. She's not exactly the most honest barmaid, but she's ... umm... resourceful."

"Seamus." Belladonna was left speechless.

"Bella, you know you don't want to be a brothel madame forever."

"Seamus."

"Bella? What is it?"

"I think I may be pregnant," Belladonna whispered to him. Seamus looked surprised.

"My darling, then you hold the grail." He grabbed her by the hand and looked for a place to protect her.

Two men spotted Seamus and ran towards him with pistols aimed. Pirates. Outlaws. Bandits. They didn't waste any time. They fired their guns at Seamus' feet. "Seamus McGee, you owe us a sack of gold and we ain't waiting any longer for it."

Belladonna swept him inside and up a secret set of stairs hidden in back.

"Well hello there, my Gypsy Rose," one of the men shimmied up next to me. The smell of him revolted me. It was booze and lots of it, on his breath and his clothes. "You're new, aren't you?" He sniffed my neck very invasively, but realizing where I was, I had no choice but to play the part. I put up with it but my eyes were filled with disgust. "Mmm mmm. You smell mighty purdy. Like a fresh picked flower. A pink rosebud."

"Hey, we ain't got no time for that, yet. Seamus went inside," he began as he stepped inside. He yelled, "Hey Seamus McGee. We know you're in here and we ain't leavin' 'til you pay us good."

Several of the girls stopped serving the tables and stared. One of the bandits snagged a whiskey shot glass off the table and slugged it back. He handed it to the other bandit. That one took the shot glass in hand and crushed it, the same way we'd crush a soda pop can to be recycled. He growled an "Arrrggh" sound as he let the piece of glass fall to the floor and revealed a bloody hand to the crowd.

I winced to see such a display of stupidity. Obviously though he had an impact on the other girls in the tavern. They clung to one another scared.

"And there's a lotta purdy girls in here. Wouldn't want any of dem to get hurt, if you catch my drift, Seamus. Git down here and be a man and show yerself."

Seamus burst through an upper doorway at the top of the stairs. In his hands, he clutched a sack. The rope around its neck bulged. He held it at the neck over the railing.

"Aye, that's a good lad. Wouldn't want anyone to get hurt now do we? Toss it down 'ere." The bounty hunter greedily licked his lips.

"As ye wish." Seamus tossed the sack. It went airborne over the railing of the stairs and towards the tavern floor. It landed sloppily and spilt its shimmering golden contents over the floor and atop tables, sending poker cards and chips flying into the air alongside of it. The Queen of Hearts card landed right at my feet. I picked it up and tucked it inside of my corset.

"Gold!" someone yelled.

"Mine!" another yelled.

A stein of beer got flung into the air and it crashed down and broke into jagged pieces. A barmaid bent down to pick up the pieces of porcelain from the stein and she was goosed by one of the patrons. He let out a drunken laugh.

"Hey. Hands off the ladies," Wendy shouted at the man. "Yer not allowed to be touchin' the ladies 'nless they escort ye to one o' our private rooms."

He stood drunkenly out of his chair and attempted to grab at the barmaid, but missed. He landed face first on the floor, flat as a pancake and did not get up. Wendy shrugged her shoulders and turned to face the main area of the barkeep. A man had climbed the balcony and outstretched his arms, reaching for the chandelier, which was an old carriage wheel turned on its side. He grabbed at it and managed to grasp one edge of the wheel. He swung it back and forth before jumping down onto a table top, making every beer stein on the table jump up a few good inches before settling back down and splashing over. He reached down and grabbed a stein off the table and swigged it back.

Several men took the liberty of ignoring the house rules. They jumped the bartop and attacked the bartender, stealing bottles of booze and sampling shots. A rogue bent one of the girl's back over his arm into a dip. He stole a kiss from her and breaths later he swept another girl on his right into his arms and kissed her! A gal in each arm!

"Hold ye horses! Kissing the ladies 'ill be costin' ye extra, ye know and doncha be thinkin' I'm not keepin' a tab on each of ye," Wendy shouted over the bar. A man dressed in black rushed towards Wendy and swept her up off the floor and carried her over to the bartop and sat her down and kissed her. She punched him square across the jaw and sent him spilling to the floor. She hopped down from the bartop.

Within moments, the crowd in the tavern looked like squirrels fighting over peanuts. Fists began to fly. The tavern was filled with drunk monkeys all dressed as pirates and gangsters and rogues. The girls were screaming as they dizzily ran about the room in the mayhem. Seamus grabbed Belladonna by the hand and led her down the stairs swiftly during the diversion, walking in a manner that covered her belly with him sidestepping in front of her. They escaped out the front door and ran in the direction of the horse tied to the post.

Wendy didn't waste any time in putting an end to the disturbance in the tavern. She punched out the bandit and took his pistol and shot it up into the air. A pigeon hiding up in the ceiling flew out unexpectedly and exploded a cluster of grey feathers falling to the floor.

"Now who's next? What 're ye? A pack a wild coyotes? Git outta my tavern or I'll shoot the first set a spurs that scuffs me floor and lasso ye with yer own whips!" she spat into the crowd. The crowd paused, including two girls caught in a hair pull with one another.

The bandit sat up. He held his head briefly before falling back over.

"Hey, dis ain't real gold. Dis is *Fool's Gold*," the bandit with the bleeding hand said as he picked up a painted coin. It had been brushed with pyrite. He bit the coin and revealed it to be made of nickel. "May as well be a wooden nickel!"

"Hey. We've been duped. Seamus! I'm gonna get you! You've got a date with the gallows!" the bandit shouted up at the stairwell. He hadn't noticed Seamus' exit.

I peeked outside to see Seamus help Belladonna up on the horse. It was a golden and beige coloured horse with its wild mane flowing like shafts of wheat. Belladonna struggled briefly and he caught her footing. He climbed up behind her and kicked the horse in the side as he slapped the reins. "YA!" he shouted. Belladonna held tightly around Seamus' waist. The horse let out a whinny and shot off with a start down the alley and out of view. I wasn't sure whether I'd be seeing them again, at least in the current time I'd been thrown into.

Two men ran out of the tavern past me, slapping the wooden doors back against me. I let out a winch of pain and complaint.

"Hey, watch it!" I yelled at them.

I left the tavern and began walking in the direction Seamus and Belladonna fled. The horse hoof prints were left in the dust and dirt of the path and as I walked I wiped each away with my own so they would not be followed by the bandits. The music of the tavern faded behind me. As I walked, I meditated and became lost in my own thoughts. I hadn't noticed the hoof prints just disappeared from the path, as though the horse took flight.

She's pregnant. She's pregnant with – with Lily. I thought about the bandits. I already knew what would happen in the future. I knew, but Belladonna didn't. I knew that Seamus would eventually be killed and Lily would be raised by an evil queen. But this is the 1800's. Prince Ivan and Lily were from the 1600's. How did Belladonna go back two hundred years? It occurred to me that she went back the same way I just went back. Belladonna learned to create a portal.

I stopped to hear an owl. I looked around and noticed the western town had disappeared. I was back in a forest. The owl sat upon a tree just in front of me. It was Henry. *Hoot. Hoot. Hoooooooooooooot.*

"Henry!" I called to the owl, hoping it might somehow recognize me and speak as so many of my pets had.

No sooner than I'd said it, I found myself back in the treehouse with Ethan snoring next to me. It was present day again. The leap back into my present day body felt unusual, almost like falling hard into a suction cup.

"Welcome back," Abigail said. "Don't worry about the side effects of gravity. The astral world can sometimes be disorienting when you're first learning to fly. You'll get used to them as you learn to portal through time."

"Abigail, I really wish you'd give me some warning next time."

"Did you think we used brooms?" she asked with honest eyes.

"No, no of course not," I said with an unsure laugh.

"You already know the story of Seamus and the Black Widow. But there is still more you must learn from your past life, and mine. This time though, it is up to you to create the portal. You know how, even if you don't think you do. Perhaps there is something in the book that may help you." She smiled and took a step back into the doorway of the treehouse. "I suggest you rest though, before you try to fly again. You will arrive in the same bodily condition as you left. If you are weak, you will be unprepared for what awaits. Prepare yourself." She transformed into the white raven and flew off.

Fly? The book? The sacred book of the seven sisters? That book? The book in the secret room? I'd have to go back.

I looked at Ethan sleeping peacefully. He grunted as he snored. I laid down beside him and stared up at the ceiling, reflecting on everything I'd just learned, – and seen. It wasn't a dream. Two things occurred to me. I'd traveled through time, broomstick or not, and I'd killed a man.

Chapter 4

THE BLACK OWL RETURNS

eing a witch sometimes felt confusing. Add to that being a teenage girl and I had all sorts of problems to deal with. I knew I had magical abilities; I just didn't know how to use them and the ones I had I didn't know how to control. Or at least I didn't think I could. I had to learn to trust. Something Abigail had tried to convince me of but I still had difficulty with. Trust in my own abilities. They are strong and powerful.

I looked at Ethan, who lay peacefully sleeping. "I don't need to look in the book. I can do this. I'll just focus on the stopwatch and it'll happen."

I opened the stopwatch and stared at it. I waited for the hypnotic gaze to happen. I waited a little more. The mirrored lid blurred and I found myself looking beyond the mirror and into somewhere just beyond it. Memories trapped in time. I guess I hadn't specified to what time I wanted to return. Maybe that was in the book Abigail wanted me to read.

The sound of an owl hooting thrice broke my focus. Being in the treehouse was the last thing I remember before being pulled into a vortex. I looked to my feet. My surroundings had changed. Miles of grass and dirt spread in all directions and I stood against a lonely oak tree. I stood underneath it and looked up through its branches. It was the largest oak tree I'd ever seen. The air around me had an electrical charge. I thought of Ethan for a moment, and the plasma ball we'd played with in his bedroom. How our hands touched and the streams of lightning inside the ball joined together. I wondered if Ethan was safe left behind in the treehouse. Lightning struck the surrounding area. I jumped back.

There was an unusual smell of burning wood in the air, but not of the fresh firewood smell, more like charred flesh. It smelled of an odd electrical ozone smell, like sulfur or a metallic...very unpleasant. I stepped back a few feet from the tree and looked up at it. It was completely split down the center. Lightning had just struck it. I looked at it helplessly, wondering if the tree would die before me like a victim innocently caught in the crossfire. The ground around me felt like it went into shock. It vibrated into me through my toes and I felt like my body was a copper wire grounding itself into the earth.

Another bolt of lightning touched down to the ground not far from the tree. I looked around to run, but there was nothing. Only a large stretch of land and a lone tree. It looked to be plotted out for building a house.

I stood with my back against the tree. There was no place to go. I couldn't run. I prayed the lightning wouldn't strike twice on the tree.

"Hello?" a girl's voice spoke.

I looked around. There was no one around the tree but me. I walked the base of it. It was probably five or six feet in diameter; rather large for a tree stuck out in the middle of nowhere.

"You there. You are Alyson, are you not?" the voice asked.

"Who's there?"

"You will see," the voice spoke. It came from the tree this time.

I peeked around the tree with lightning still splashing all around it in all directions. "Where are you?"

"I'm right here."

There was no one visible. "I can't see you."

"No one can," she said.

"Well how do I know what you look like?"

"I look the same to this tree as your soul does to your body," she answered. "You will not be able to see me until you can see auras." She paused. "Even then, you will only be able to see colours. I have been told I am, oh, what's the word you humans use? Yellow."

"I see."

"Not yet."

"No, I mean, I understand."

"You will."

I was confused, talking with a tree. However, being miles from anywhere else and unsure how to get back to the present time, I continued my conversation.

A strong part of me felt connected with this tree. It was familiar to me. And her riddles made me want to ask her more questions.

The lightning stopped and the skies turned to blue.

"There. That's better. Now do you see me?"

I concentrated hard in the area surrounding the tree. From behind the tree stepped a yellow transparent silhouette of a girl. She had no features. She glowed and shimmered.

"I do see you!"

"Yes, of course you do. You see energy. Look. I can change elements." Her transparent energy glowed and then shifted until I saw a figure made of fire. Her silhouette glowed like a candle flame. As quickly as she was a flame she changed to water. From water to air. And from air to earth. She became a tree, rather a human made with skin of bark. Barkskin. Then she took on her spirit form and became the yellow glowing energy again.

"Amazing!"

"I can teach you," she started. "It is sacred knowledge that I am permitted to teach to my sisters."

"Your sisters?"

"Yes. Including you."

"Wait. I've never asked your name."

"Always remember that names have power, dear sister, and sacred knowledge should be sacredly taught. If you are unwilling to accept this oath, I shant tell you my name. But if you vow to use your gifts only for the good of humankind, then I will whisper it to you."

"I do accept."

"Very well. Then you may call me Rowen."

"Rowen."

"My sister. One day this tree, this magnificent tree will be chopped down because they assume it is dead. They assume it has no life inside of it anymore. They forget that the tree is the most connected living thing on earth. It connects the ground and sky. Inside every tree lives a spirit. Just because the tree that houses it dies, does not mean the spirit dies, as is the same of your body. It is merely flesh and it too will die. But you will not. If you have not learned this already, it will become clear to you as you learn the destiny of your soul."

"The destiny of my soul?"

"On top of this most hallowed ground, a house will be built. The house is your house. It is also the house of Sadie Finch, who will discover my spells and learn how to manipulate lightning and other elements. Sadie was first to discover my sacred knowledge."

"But if you can see this happening in the future, why don't you stop it?"

"I can't. We must make mistakes in order to learn from them. Besides, it is because of Sadie's lightning that causes her to become a ghost. It is a power she learned that helps her travel to the underworld. It is also a power that will help her defeat Hremm Nevar and other demons. Unbeknownst to many, Sadie is one of the most powerful of her kind."

I paced around the base of the tree. "But the lightning? Didn't it just strike the tree?"

"Yes. Several times."

"But lightning doesn't strike the same place more than once, does it?"

"It does here. This is no ordinary tree, Alyson. You should know why already."

I didn't. I was supposed to have all of this sacred knowledge already and I didn't. I hesitated asking. I was eager as a sponge ready to absorb whatever she had to whisper to me.

"Umm. Refresh my memory?"

The yellow energy shape reached forward and touched my forehead.

"Ouch!" I yelped and held my forehead in pain. "What did you do?"

"I refreshed your memory," she said.

After several seconds, the pain cleared. Images far below the ground and inside the earth began to grow in my mind's eye. Fiery lava, salt, rock layers, hidden oasis's. And something dark, and black. A hole.

"What is that?" I questioned.

"In the universe, it is known as a wormhole. It is the opposite side of a black hole. Because of the location of this tree, it can exist in several realms at once. Here, time travel is possible. Into the future or the past, as above, so below. This tree sits upon a portal between the realms. It is a sacred tree. And soon, the tree will fall and a house will be built. That house is now your house and you must listen to it carefully for it speaks to you. It will be built from the wood of this tree. It is sacred wood. It is a wood that will never die. The spirit remains within. Lightning continually strikes down this tree, but an acorn will grow it again, over and over. The cycle is never broken."

"My house. A sacred house?"

"Your house has a mind's eye of its own – an astral treehouse if it were."

"The secret room in the attic."

"It's not a secret any more. Others have divulged of its location."

"Who?"

"I cannot tell you."

"Why not?"

"I grow tired of questions. I only have so much energy to lend to you. It is up to you to replenish mine."

"Well how do I do that?"

"Goodbye, Alyson." She faded.

"Okay, well fine," I said, miffed and impatient. I yearned to know more. I felt the power my greed had taken from her, and suddenly I felt very selfish.

"Thank you, Rowen. I will do my best to understand and to keep your spirit alive."

I looked around. There was nothing. Something rolled and hit my foot. A nut. An acorn. I picked up the fallen acorn from the tree. In doing so, I heard the rolling water of a creek in the distance. "No, it can't be." *Hollow Creek*.

I listened for the sound of the creek and tried to hone in on its direction, but could not discern it with the other noises randomly distracting me. "If only I knew which direction north was."

Recalling earlier at Grams' house, she'd given me a compass. "No. It couldn't be." I reached inside my pocket. There was the compass, but the stopwatch was nowhere to be found. I had the sudden realization I didn't know how to get back home. My second thoughts reminded me of Abigail's words. "Maybe I should've read the book first," I said doubting myself.

I tried to use the compass but the electricity still radiating from the tree prevented it from doing anything but spin wildly in all directions.

"Pointless," I yelled at the compass. I took about twenty paces back from the tree. The compass stopped spinning and instead ticked back and forth like a clock pendulum, unsure of where to land. I briskly stepped back another twenty paces or so and the needle stopped and pointed north.

"Yes!" I exclaimed as I read the compass. I wondered if Grams' house had been built yet. I knew the path, but the path was not there. I'd just have to recall the steps I took if the path *were* there and walk that. It was etched in my memory.

I walked for awhile and came to Hollow Creek. No bridge had been built yet. It was too wide for me to jump it, so I scaled down the rocks and tiptoed across it. I climbed up the other side only to come face to face with Ethan. But it wasn't Ethan.

"Sorry, miss. Didn't mean to surprise you."

He had on suspenders, beige slacks and a page boy hat. He was probably in his mid teens. "That's quite a house they built back in there. Are you a friend of the Finch's?" He pointed in the direction behind me. I looked back and the scenery had changed. Trees had grown up all around and just beyond them was the famous Finch Estate, only it was very newly built.

"Umm. Yes. Well, I'm not sure. I'm a long lost relative." Technically, I wasn't lying. I really was lost.

"Oh I see. Nice to meet you. I'm Harding. Harding Danby." He put out his hand to shake mine. *Harding?* My jaw dropped.

I shook it. "It's my pleasure, good sir."

"Still working here on this stone bridge." He took off his hat and wiped sweat off his brow and I realized he stood next to a pile of stones. Cobblestones.

"Oh, Harding. Oh where, oh where are you hiding?" a cheerful singing voice came from behind. A girl with red hair came running playfully towards the creek. It was Emelia. She couldn't have been more than fifteen or sixteen.

Harding's eyes lit up. "Emelia!" He ran to her. They embraced briefly.

"Harding, not here. People will see. You know I don't like to kiss you… in public!" Emelia said embarrassedly.

"Emelia, there's no one around."

"There's a girl. We're you with another girl and didn't tell me?" she prodded.

"No, of course not. You know you're the only gal for me. This here is, umm, sorry, didn't catch your name miss," Harding yelled back to me.

I didn't throw it. I didn't know it. Odd. I couldn't think of my own name. I looked at him confused and made up the first name that came to mind. "Elisabeth. My name is Elisabeth." I felt very odd. His resemblance to Ethan was uncanny. To see him kissing Emelia really struck my core.

"Elisabeth," he said my name and it had a smile all too familiar attached to it. He reminded me of Ethan. If I didn't know better, I'd say it was. "Allow me to properly introduce you to my friend, Miss Emelia Finch."

"Pleasure to meet you, Emelia," I said to her. She had never met me before and acted as such, even though I knew of her future fate. I bit my tongue on telling her any information. My intuition told me that it would be a bad consequence to meddle with the past and alter the future. But what if Harding didn't die? What if Emelia and Harding marry? What if Sadie never meets Hremm Nevar? I had so many questions with so many possible answers. I felt my presence intrusive and decided it best to move along no matter how great my curiousity.

"Likewise miss. I don't recall seeing you around the area. Did you just move in?"

I paused for a moment to point to our house, but it was their house now, not mine. I suddenly realized I didn't know where home was. It felt sad and lost.

"I – I, I am without a home at the moment, miss," I said humbly.

"Are you an orphan? A runaway? No matter. You will come live with us now. We have a spare room in the attic you can stay in. Do you like to paint? I've been thinking of sprucing up the room with some pictures, paintings right on the wall of jungle animals and critters," Emelia rambled.

"Oh Emelia," Harding began with a laugh. "You and your wild imagination. I'd swear you were crazy if one day you didn't just up and leave for a safari in the jungles or to climb Mt. Kilimanjaro!"

I paused to reflect the possibility. The attic. The secret room. Was it there already? Would I be able to open the cupboard door? The book. I had to get to the book. "Yes. Yes, I mean, if you don't mind. I can help with chores."

"It's settled then. Harding, walk us home."

He smiled. "The pleasure is all mine, accompanying two lovely ladies for a walk on this blessed day." Harding glanced my direction and smiled. I felt the same way I did the day I met Ethan. A crush had started. What was going on?

"But what about the storm?" I asked concerned. "Has it passed?"

"Storm?" Harding looked at me questionably.

"There's been no storm. Oh dear, Harding, I wonder if she's gone and bumped her head," Emelia replied. I couldn't tell whether she was serious.

I knew the way. Only ten minutes ago I'd walked a barren path from an empty lightning split tree in the middle of nowhere. Around me, a lush forest had sprung up, and a dusty dirt path leading back down the rest of Colby Drive. The house came into view. It was just as it is now, only it had been built just over a decade ago. A light was on in the attic.

Chapter 5

REVELATIONS

melia pushed open the door with one hand. No locks had been put on the main door. She called throughout the house from the foyer, with a cheerful smile and prim manner. "Mother? Father? We have a guest with us."

George Finch came out of the study, which is now my Dad's office.

"Hello."

"Father, this is Elisabeth."

He nodded and shook my hand.

"With your permission, can she stay with us for awhile? She is without a home, or parents, and may have bumped her head. She has amnesia."

"Where are you from child?"

I paused. I didn't have an answer to give him. I honestly didn't know. I lowered my head ashamed and defeated by my own mind.

"Do you not know where you're from?"

I knew I had to come up with something to appease him. He was very stern. I was used to stern with my own father, but George Finch was not a man to trifle with.

"I umm, I was in an accident and I've lost my memory. I'm hoping it will come back soon." I glanced at a calendar hanging in the kitchen, just out of view.

September 1926.

I'd advanced 40 years in time since 1887, yet I was no older than a teenager. I looked to Emelia, who appeared to be the same age as me. My stomach went into an immediate knot when I thought of the old newspaper clippings Ethan had shown me. I remembered Harding's obituary, a fall day in October 1926. It was that same day Sadie met Hremm Nevar. One month away. I swallowed the news deeply and realized I was still in the present company of George Finch and Emelia, and Harding. My eyes shot to Harding and his caught mine. There was recognition in them.

Could it be?

"Oh. Well then of course, please stay with us," George Finch began. "In the meantime while we search for your parents, as someone must certainly be looking for you, we can provide you with shelter and warmth off the streets. You appear to be the same age as both of my daughters. Perhaps they can lend you some clothing," he said as he looked me up and down a little judging my clothing. I looked down and was wearing an outfit I hadn't seen before.

"Where is Sadie?" Emelia asked.

"Oh I think she's around back at the lake. She's got some fascination with that place."

"We'll go there next. Come Elisabeth and I will show you to your room. Harding, please wait in the foyer. What would my mother say to see you near my bedroom?" she asked, toying with him. He laughed and glanced at me. It was a glance that hinted my heart knew him more than Emelia had previously suggested. But why? She told me he was *her* true love.

"Hello, dear ones. Did someone call me?" A woman's voice emerged from the kitchen. "Oh hello. We have a guest I see." I took in a deep breath. There before me was Abigail, only this Abigail was young, much younger than the Abigail I had come to know. "You will join us for tea. Come to the kitchen. I've been expecting you."

"You have?" I looked at her surprised. I wondered if she already knew who I was and that I'd come from the future?

"Yes. Do you know how many forks I've dropped this morning?"

"Forks?" I wasn't sure what she talked about, but suspected this was what 'old wives tales' and divinations were made of.

I walked into the kitchen and looked to the table. It had four place settings, set for tea and scones. "Do be a dear and call your sister in please, Emelia."

"Harding is here as well."

"Oh, then it would be splendid if he could make his way down to the lake to get Sarah. I'm certain she's forgotten her shoes again and you know how tender-footed she is."

"Certainly mother. Harding can carry her. I will ask him."

I felt compelled to intervene, but couldn't.

"Umm, I feel a little queasy. I'll show myself to the toilet." They both looked appalled at me.

"The toilet is not meant to put one's face into. You may go outside to the back if you will. Fresh air, I find, can cure many ailments," Abigail said as she pointed me in the direction of the back door, which was now our sliding kitchen glass door. "I'll make you some tea with ginger and honey. That will cure you right up."

I fled quickly to the back of the house and peered around the corner of a wood pile. Harding's voice made a chuckle as he closed the front door behind him and headed my direction towards the lake. His resemblance to Ethan was distracting.

Harding skipped slightly as he went down the path to the lake. I knew it well. I ran to the entrance and dodged his glances by hiding behind trees. He was focused on finding Sadie.

"Peek-a-boo," a voice came from behind a tree.

"Sadie, is that you?" Harding stopped and looked around. A giggle came from behind the trees. I could not see her and neither could Harding.

She giggled again and emerged from behind the trees. She too was once again the beautiful, long raven haired beauty that I'd seen the day in the mirror. She loosened up the top of her dress and it almost fell.

She covered her smiled with her hand in false embarrassment. "I almost lost my dress. What would you do if I did?" She lowered an elasticized sleeve off her shoulder and peeked from just over it, showing him her back as she lowered the opposite side. She giggled.

"Sadie, what are you doing? We don't have time for that."

She let her dress fall to her ankles. I'd never seen such a beautiful woman naked before. I couldn't stop staring.

"Come find me, Harding," she sang as she playfully ran off between the trees and headed towards the lake.

Harding looked curious and ran off after her.

"Sadie, wait," he yelled.

"Come find me," she playfully sang through the trees. There was a splashing sound. Sadie had dove into the lake.

Harding caught up with her and stared at her peeking out from the lake's surface. She swam backwards and Harding took in a full view of her naked body. She spun around and spoke.

"Do you like what you see, Harding?"

Harding didn't speak, but he didn't leave either. I continued to hide behind a tree.

"Sadie, I – I," he stumbled on his words.

She flirtatiously swam like a sea nymph or a water goddess. He was mesmerized by her and could not look away.

"Come into the water, my darling. My Harding," she sang.

He stood there in deliberation.

"I won't bite," she began and giggled, "but I might nibble." He clearly became tempted by her. His eyes locked onto her. Temptress as she was, she moved her body back and forth in the water, making waves disturbing the surface so he could not peer clearly through it. Her breasts peek-a-boo'd just above the water before going beneath again and cleverly hid by her dark hair. Harding nearly lost his footing. He took a step backwards and leaned his arm heavily against a tree.

"Sadie, I – I can't," he stammered. He seemed to be convincing himself. He looked at her once again and then looked away.

She looked upset. "Well if you won't, then I'm going to dive underwater and I'm not coming up until you come out to get me!" she threatened.

"Sadie. You most certainly will not do such behavior. Why, I am appalled at your rather vulgar display of your... umm... nakedness. Imagine what your mother would say if I told her how you behaved this moment."

Sadie looked furious and flaunted herself while Harding pretended to shield his eyes.

"I will not look at you, Sadie. You will not succeed in seducing me with your – your," he stuttered as he glanced at her again and then looked away. "Your -," he started again but did not finish. Sadie dove underwater, mooning him with her buttocks as she disappeared below. The surface of the water rippled above her and then went still.

"Sadie, come now. Your mother requests your presence for tea," Harding yelled through the water. Sadie did not surface. Several moments passed. Harding took steps closer to the water's edge.

"Sadie! Stop this childish behavior at once!" he commanded in his deepest voice of a boy of seventeen years. Still, she did not surface. The look on Harding's face changed to worry.

"Sadie? ... Sadie?"

No response.

"Well, I'll be damned. She's gone and drowned herself!" He flung off his cap and shoes before diving into the water himself.

Moments passed. He emerged from the surface holding a limp and naked Sadie.

He carried her to the shore of the lake and set her on the ground.

"Sadie? Speak to me. Sadie?" He shook her shoulders and lightly slapped the sides of her face. He didn't wait for her to respond. "Sadie, you can't drown on me."

He pinched her nose and covered her mouth with his and prepared to blow to resuscitate. Her hand reached up and slipped behind his neck and held him locked in an unwarranted kiss. He'd kissed her for several moments before he realized what he'd done. A rustling of leaves on the forest floor alerted Harding they were no longer alone. He looked back to the path.

"How dare you!?" a voice came from behind me on the path. "Sadie! You immoral wretch! How dare you?"

"And you, Harding! How dare you be so intimate with my sister, my own flesh and blood! I cannot believe my own eyes. My sister, naked and laying in a bed of leaves! Harding! I demand the truth at once!"

"She – she had drowned. I was saving her. I was saving her life," he pleaded.

Emelia pondered for a moment whether to believe him.

"He lies Emelia! He lies! He threw himself upon me and tore off my dress. He's a monster Emelia! He has no self control. You should leave him at once!" Sadie lied.

"She lies. She steals! She stole a kiss from me. I would never kiss you Sadie, not in another ten thousand years! To kiss you is to kiss a ghost, for you will be dead before you ever steal from me again! You have no soul and no shame, you – you, harlot!" He picked up her dress and threw it at her. It landed in a ruffled pile around her midsection.

Sadie laughed. Harding narrowed his eyes.

"I do not believe you. You only wish someone would come here and tear off your clothes, you – you conniving and despicable little whore!" Emelia spat. Sadie gasped and then grinned as her sister swore. Harding looked shocked too.

"Don't forget your cap, soldier boy." She laughed. Emelia knew instantly she'd been lied to.

"Come Harding. Sadie doesn't deserve to sit with us for tea today. She's clearly gone and lost her mind and whatever little dignity she once had!" Emelia spat at Sadie as she walked in arm and arm with Harding with her nose stuck up high in the air.

None of them saw me. Sadie got up from the ground and slipped on her dress. She looked satisfied. She'd implanted the seed of doubt in Emelia's mind. As I watched Sadie, I recalled a memory from the present time. Ethan and Carly. She too had planted a seed of doubt in my mind.

I debated following Harding and Ethan or staying behind to watch what Sadie would do next. Sadie moved aside a rock from the ground and got on her hands and knees. I decided to stay hidden behind the tree and watch her. From underneath the rock there was a hole. She reached her hands inside and pulled out a box, opening it.

From inside the box, she pulled out a book. It was her spellbook – one I'd seen before in the future.

A raven squawked, and another one. Several ravens landed in the surrounding trees. The air contained a new chill as a breeze passed through.

Sadie cracked open the book and thumbed the pages.

"Let's see, let's see. A ha! A spell for true love."

From past and present and future times
Send me a soul mate that matches mine
Let him recognize me by my eyes
And only see others disguised
I wish, I wish, I wish
For him to be Har—Hrm...

Sadie gasped as the sound startled her. Her spell had been interrupted by the sound of lightning. A raven let out a call. *Squawk. Squawwwwwk. Squawk.*

"Thrice the raven beckons again. It has been cast. Oh no. The spells been cast, but who did it cast on?" she panicked. "Did I cast it on Harding?"

We both heard the sounds of people coming. It was Abigail, Harding and Emelia. I methodically positioned myself around the back of the tree so as not to be seen by either party.

"She's down there," Harding shouted and pointed in the direction of the lake.

Sadie quickly scrambled to put her dress back on. She then sat on a rock as though she were lost in deep meditation. Her acting reminded me distinctly of my present day schoolmate Sara's.

"Sarah? Sarah, darling? Are you alright?" Abigail yelled as she hurriedly ran down the hill towards the lake, her dress flowing behind her.

"Mother. I – I am here. I am fine," she said as she saw Harding return. She smiled at Harding and gave him a wink.

"Hardly," Emelia spat at her. Sadie stuck out her tongue in retort.

"Girls behave yourselves. You're in the company of a gentleman. Now Sadie, if you are done swimming, kindly gather yourself and join us inside for tea. Your presence is noticeably missed, darling."

"Yes, Mother. I will be there momentarily. Please allow me a few minutes to recompose myself, in private. I was merely meditating when so rudely interrupted by my dear sister and her accompaniment."

"Sarah, did you not hear the lightning? A storm will be here soon. We all must return inside at once," Abigail insisted and held out her hand to help Sadie. "Bring your book."

Sadie looked stunned. She wanted to keep her book a secret, but did as she was instructed. Reluctantly, Sadie followed suit up the footpath and back into the house. I waited a moment, hugging myself carefully around the tree and moving as they moved, so they would not see me behind it. Once they returned inside, I crept in through the front door.

I paused for a moment at the base of the stairwell. I had the choice of either joining the group, or exploring a house I knew all too familiarly. It was a hard decision. As much as I wanted to stay and see the interaction between the sisters and Harding, I felt like a spy. I knew I had to get back to my own time. The secret room in the attic was my only hope.

I quietly ran up the stairwell to the upper floor where the bedrooms were and ran to the hallway table. The familiar grandfather clock that stood in the corner chimed five o'clock pm. It would be dark soon. I stood in front of the table. I looked underneath it and pressed the wall as I had done in my own time and crept inside. The stairwell recognized me and I found myself at the top without taking a single step. It felt as though I'd flown up them.

To my right was the extra bedroom, the one I knew I'd be staying in. But the bedroom was not my interest at the moment. I looked to the cupboard which disguised the secret room.

I opened the cupboard door and peeked inside, ready to enter the secret room and find my way back to Ethan in the treehouse. The cupboard door opened, but it was not the secret room.

There were nothing but linen towels and wash rags. It smelled of pure soap and the intensity of it made me sneeze.

I stood bewildered. *How do I find the secret room now? Does it even exist yet?*

Disappointed I walked down the stairs and exited the tiny doorway underneath the table. Footsteps began rising the stairwell. It was Emelia.

"Elisabeth. I had wondered where you'd toddled off to." She noticed the proximity to where I stood in relationship to the table. Her mind held questions but she did not ask them.

"I – I was just looking for you actually. I thought maybe you had come up to your room." Instinctively my finger pointed to her door which now was my bedroom, as a visibly faint trail of a white blue light made its way to the door. There was the sound of a 'click' and the knob on the door turned. It swung wide open without so much as the help of my hand turning it.

Emelia just stood there with her mouth as open as the door.

I felt mine equally so. I had powers.

Chapter 6

FOREWARNING

melia stuttered as she stared at her open door. "How did you – how did you do that?"

I wanted to tell her but I didn't know. It just happened. I pointed my finger at the door and it opened. But it was more than just pointing my finger. The wish was there in my heart behind it. That's where the spell was.

"Are you a – a Witch?" she asked directly.

I hesitated responding. She didn't look pleased at the idea, but she also had such curiousity in her eyes that I wanted to tell her. More so, I wanted to show her – to show her what I knew so that she could stay protected from Sadie and what was to come. But I knew I couldn't. This was beyond me and would be considered meddling in others lives. I would be reprimanded for it, I was sure of it. Before I could respond, we both heard footsteps approaching.

Abigail walked up the stairwell, pausing for a moment to take notice of my presence so close to the table. It stirred her. She knew! Magic was in the air and she felt it.

I wanted to run back up to the secret room and try again to open it. I felt certain I'd be able to if I'd only put my mind to it. Some tasks just required ultimate concentration.

"Elisabeth, please join us downstairs for tea. Emelia will lend you a dress to wear," she began. "Emelia dear, please do not keep Harding and your sister waiting. Make haste."

"Mother?" Emelia looked at Abigail like she'd just discovered oil for the first time.

"Yes dear? What is it?"

"It's okay Emelia. I think the door just opened on its own. There's a draft nearby. Bet there's a window open somewhere that opened it, or a cross breeze, from that bedroom." I refrained from pointing my finger at Sadie's closed bedroom door.

Emelia nodded, uncertain whether to believe her own intuition or not.

Abigail smiled and didn't say anything. She descended back down the stairwell. Her thoughts concerned me. Did she know?

Emelia still looked stunned. She finally accepted whatever answer she was most satisfied with. "Very well then."

Emelia showed me her room and I pretended not to be familiar with it. "It's a nice room. I like the picture window. It would be a nice place to sit and read a book."

"Yes, well actually," she started but then hesitated. She glanced at the wooden chest nestled in the book nook. The chest had the familiar lock on it; the lock I'd open with the key I'd find in Dad's library. Inside that chest resided Emelia's spellbook. I walked over to the window seat and sat down. I sensed the book's presence beneath me. It wasn't well shielded.

Emelia pulled a dress from out of her closet and held it up to me. "This will fit you. Try it on." I took the dress and slid it over my head. Emelia tied the tassels in the back and cinched the waist. I felt curvy.

We ran down the stairs to find Harding and Sadie sitting opposite one another. She openly and shamelessly flirted with him, while he rejected her advances and seemed repulsed and disgusted at the idea of her kissing him. He licked his lips subconsciously. He desired her. He looked up at Emelia and then to me. Once again, our glance left a curiosity behind it that made us both uncomfortable. Emelia, in her suspicions, noticed the way our eyes met.

"Emelia. Elisabeth. Come join us. Please have a seat." Harding stood up and pulled out two chairs for each of us to sit down in. He waited for each of us to sit and then pushed in our chairs, resuming his position in his own chair.

"Do you two, know each other?" Emelia directed the question to Harding and me. Harding seemed perplexed and uncertain.

"I can't place it. I feel like we've met before, miss," he said. It gave me shivers.

"I believe that might be impossible," I attempted to explain. I felt it might be wisest not to say anything more. Emelia gave me jealous glances. She wasn't the Emelia of the present, but rather a very self-conscious teenage girl. Actually, she reminded me of myself a little, before Ethan entered my life, and coincidentally, when the magic began to unfold.

Sadie snickered. "Looks like you've got even more competition, Emelia," Sadie whispered to her sister without Harding overhearing. Emelia's forehead furled.

Abigail entered the room with a full tray of cakes and tea cups. Harding stood to his feet again and pulled out a chair for Abigail to sit. She smiled and thanked him.

"Let us thank the good Lord for watching over us, and for blessing our bounty."

"Amen," Harding said with a quiet smile. Emelia followed suit. Sadie said Amen too, but then stuck out her tongue at her sister.

Emelia stuck her tongue out right back.

"Emelia Rosemarie Finch! Such very unladylike behavior in front of a gentleman!" Abigail snapped.

"But Sadie," Emelia began.

"But nothing. You sisters will behave yourselves. We have a guest here in our presence."

I gulped so loudly that everyone heard through the silence. They looked at me with curious eyes. I'm sure they wondered who I was and where I was from, almost as much as I did. Unfortunately, they didn't have any answers that would assist me. I dabbed my white cloth napkin against my lips and cleared my throat.

We sat silently and sipped our tea. I'd hoped for more conversation, but anytime anyone attempted to speak, Abigail reminded us to be quiet. It was an unusual ceremony, very old fashioned, prim and proper.

In the silence, I kept my head down. Every time I lifted it, Harding stared at me. The last time, I let a smile show. Even if this was my Ethan, he didn't know it. I wasn't supposed to be a part of this time. I came here by accident. Harding and Emelia were meant to be together and in one month's time, he's going to ask her hand in marriage. As hard as it was, I knew my presence stirred something in Harding, something that confused him. I had to leave.

"Abigail – I mean, Mrs. Finch, may I talk with you in private?"

"Yes certainly, Elisabeth. Let us go into the greenhouse. Please excuse us for one moment," she told to Emelia and Harding as she showed me the way, although every inch of the house was already very familiar to me.

"How may I help you?" she asked.

I paused. I had so many things to say and ask. I didn't know much about Abigail prior to her carriage accident, which would happen three years from now. Maybe I should give her a warning? How could I? What could I tell her that wouldn't sound completely as though I'd gone mad? I also found it discomforting knowing the future of someone's fate. Was it my job to intervene? No. I accepted that although I had knowledge I could share, I chose not to, even if it meant Abigail's death. Because I knew it was in her death that she was able to be reborn and heal others. If the death didn't happen, she might not have the ability.

"I – I just wanted to say thank you."

"Silly dear, you didn't have to pull me away in private to tell me that." She smiled and dead headed some marigolds. "Here, keep these. You can grow other flowers with these seeds."

Her voice grew older. As she placed them in my palm, she said, "You have learned what you came to learn and sought what you came to seek. You have the seeds of knowledge. Now plant them."

I felt confused. She did know. It was pointless to worry. She already knows. In my other hand, she placed the stopwatch.

"I found this outside. It does not belong to any of us. It must be yours. Perhaps holding it in your palm will remind you of someone you love and bring you back to them. It does, doesn't it?"

"Yes."

"Then your love is true. Even time cannot keep you apart." I thought of Ethan and glanced back in the direction of Harding. Seeing him here confused me. I wondered if ever there was a time before that I had known Ethan. Sometime in the past?

I looked at her curiously, and opened the lid. Gazing upon the clock, time began to spin backwards.

"To your own time return!" she commanded me and her finger pointed straight at my third eye. As it tingled, I felt myself being dragged backward through the universe.

Chapter 7

AN OUTCRY OF JUSTICE

ever was I more surprised than the moment I opened the stopwatch and found myself back in 1887. I looked around dizzily. Above me resembled a circus tent, and various carnival acrobatics happened around me. Ethan was nowhere in sight. Noise overwhelmed me.

"Abigail must've gotten confused. This isn't the 21st century?!" I bantered quietly just under my breath. As usual, the stopwatch had disappeared from my hands. "Now what do I do?"

I walked around the backstage of the circus. Ring leaders, clowns, belly dancers, and a myriad of animals all dressed in ornate costumes. Grand beasts of all sorts paraded in front of me doing acrobats. The elephants caught my eye.

"It's an amazing two-ring circus, don't you agree?" a clown with her dog approached me. "It'd be really amazing if they added a third ring. I can see this circus having a huge following. Just imagine it – a three-ring circus! How adventurous!"

"Umm, yes," I began awkwardly with a laugh, and attempted to play along. "Life sure is different here under the big top."

"Yes. Isn't it exciting? Can't you just feel the energy in the air? I find when there are lots of people and the band is playing and there's just so much happiness in the air. Can't you feel it?"

"Umm, sure."

"It's like when I got Buster here. This here is Buster Brown. He's the best dog ever and never has anyone ever seen a smarter dog that can do more tricks."

Buster stood on his hind legs and danced around. He had on a tutu and ballet slippers on his hind feet.

"That's really clever," I said and applauded. I realized I wanted to introduce myself, but once again, stumbled upon my own identity. Things were different in the past, and I'm certain my name was too. I hadn't had anyone here call me Alyson yet. In fact, no one had called me anything.

She reached out to shake my hand. I took it and shook it. "It's a pleasure to meet you. I'm Constanzie. Are you one of the gypsy girls they hired? I hear they're good." She leaned in to whisper. "I hear they are traveling with an actual seer."

I smiled. I can only guess she referred to Abigail, or Belladonna as she is known in this life.

"Belladonna?"

"Yes. That is the one. She is so wise and beautiful. I bet she can tell you who you're going to fall in love with. She is practicing to read tarot cards, but doesn't seem very good at it though. But she reads palms very well."

Recalling the gypsy reading my palm at the RenFest, I agreed. "Yes."

"So you know of her?"

"Yes."

"And who are you?"

"I am," I said with a pause, "Elisabeth – Elisabeth Welch." I hadn't known my last name previously. It just popped into my head.

"I like you, Elisabeth. I hope we become good friends."

Buster barked.

The sounds of an animal in pain came from behind us. A trainer prodded at an elephant with a rod.

"Oh, I can't stand to watch it when they do that. Come on. Let's leave."

"Wait. Shouldn't we stop him?" I asked.

"What do you mean? He's a man. You don't stop... *a man*."

"Hey there. Take it easy on that poor gal. She's a momma," a man about my age stepped in and spoke up to the elephant trainer.

"She won't listen. I'll make her listen," the trainer growled.

"Over my dead body you will," the man lunged at the trainer. The trainer whipped his rod at the man and sent him to the ground. He pulled it back full throttle into what looked like a swing of a golf club and swung. The man rolled quickly enough on the ground to avert getting his head pummeled off.

Whistles blew through the air and police came running into the big top.

"Let's move closer," Constanzie pulled me. "Keep quiet Buster." She tucked him under her arm.

I looked at the two men and my jaw dropped. There before me stood astonishing look a likes of Jeremy Fox and Ethan, my Ethan. Mr. Ethan Reilly, my dream date of the present, existed back in the 1800's? So did Jeremy Fox.

"They're both really handsome, aren't they? I love to watch men fight," Constanzie peered around a curtain at them. "I hope the trainer gets it. He deserves what he dishes out. You know, what goes around comes around – threefold?"

"Who is the man fighting the trainer?"

"Oh that's Jonathan. Jonathan Tarlington ...."

Jonathan Tarlington? Why did I not remember his name?

"Can you introduce me to him?"

"Well sure. If he doesn't get arrested," she added.

"What's the trainer's name?"

"I'm not sure. Some wandering soul they found drunk upside of a train, smelling of whisky and hadn't had a bath in near over a month. They offered him a job here, but things have been foul with him around ever since."

"I can imagine. That poor elephant."

The elephant's calf came into view and stood nestled between the legs of its mother, sheltered underneath the layers of fat protecting her.

"It's adorable. Just look into her eyes. She has an old soul," I mentioned.

"An old soul?" Constanzie asked.

"Yes. I can't explain it. It's something I'm just learning about myself. You know, the life of a soul. Or rather, the lives of a soul?"

"Oh, like how many past lives you've had? Is this a gypsy thing?"

"Yes, kinda. Maybe. I'm not really sure."

"Belladonna is good for that. She read my palm and said that I was relatively a new soul. But she told me she is very old. She wouldn't tell me how old, but I suspect it's a really long time. Maybe even Biblical times old, if you know what I mean."

The police escorted the trainer away in handcuffs.

"Fascinating!" she gasped.

"What?"

"I've never seen a man in those things before. Those, metal rings around his wrists. What do you call them?"

"Handcuffs."

"Oh yes. They are a great new invention, don't you think? Much stronger than rope and quicker to put on criminals."

New? A new invention? Oh. I had to remind myself this was the 1800's and not the present time. A lot was different. A lot was still being discovered. It was in that moment that I realized I was in the prime time of the Wild West and the Gold Rush.

"Ladies? I couldn't help but notice you over here." Jonathan walked closer to us. "Can I trouble you for a drink of water?"

"Sure," I said, ladling out a scoop of water from a bucket and pouring it into a glass. I handed it to him and he took it cautiously, so not to spill. "You look real thirsty."

"Thank you. I am, miss." He guzzled the glass of water and handed it back to me empty. I refilled it again and handed him another.

"That was really nice of you to stop that trainer from harming that mother elephant," I said.

He blushed modestly. "It was nothing. He had it coming to him. He'd done it before. No animal should have to go through the punishment of a man's hand in the name of entertainment."

"You are so compassionate. That's rare," Constanzie said. Jonathan looked at her the way Ethan looked at Carly.

"I do try, miss. It is miss, isn't it?" he flirted.

Constanzie shyly flirted back with her eyelashes and not saying a word.

I heavily debated what to do. Was this Ethan? Should I intervene? I debated the consequences of messing with my own destiny and deemed it appropriate to wait to see what would happen if fate brought us together again, alone.

I left the tent discreetly unnoticed. I trusted that if Ethan was meant for me then he'd come find me. I held confidently in my heart that fate would bring us together. It had to. Or I was doomed.

I walked around the circle of wagons in the caravan outside of the big top. I watched the sun go down. At dusk, I walked around back to the stables where the horses were kept. Gypsy Epona was there, Belladonna's horse. She was in her own stall now and sleeping. I walked over to her and started petting her long nose and between her eyes, on a white star conveniently placed as though it were painted on her forehead.

"You sure are a beautiful girl," I spoke to her. "Want some carrots? I'll bring some next time."

"Who said that?" a young man's voice spoke from inside one of the stalls.

"I did."

"Who is I?" he spoke again, this time standing up. It was Ethan, *or at least his look-a-like.*

I smiled at him. "Who is *I*, you ask?" We both laughed. "*I am* Elisabeth."

"That is a beautiful name, Elisabeth. Hey. You were the girl with Stanzie?"

I nodded. He *had* noticed me. "Are you in the habit of trying to charm all of the girls at this carnival?"

"Well no, of course not," he started, "only the pretty ones." He flashed me a quirky smile.

"And you must be – ?"

"Jonathan." He stuck a pitchfork into the ground and stood against it. Sweat clung to his shirt.

"Oh. Oh, you work here? In the stables?"

"I do. It's a good living. I may get a horse one day too. Got my eye on a black one over there. It's got some champion blood lines running through its veins. Royalty. But it won't tame up to no one 'cept me. I can't ride it, yet. But one day, I will and I'll be out of here and headed west. That's where all the gold is. That and up north."

Belladonna came into the stables and over to Gypsy Epona. "There's my girl." She petted her the same way I had, and had brought carrots. She smiled at me. Her belly was swollen. She was pregnant and could be due any moment. It had been several months since I saw her last the day she left the brothel and fled with Seamus.

"Stable boy. Please see if you can't be more careful with where you leave your pitchfork. One might think you're not hard at work and have to hire another," Bella spoke sternly.

"As you wish, Madame," he replied and with a swift hand took the fork from out of the hay and got back to work.

She gave him a look of displeasure. "Please. Just call me Bella."

She directed her eyes on me. "You? You were the girl I met outside the saloon several months back, weren't you?"

"Yes. You remember me?" I asked carefully.

"You look familiar. What are you skilled at?"

"Lots of things. I'm a seamstress. I can mend and sew garments, spin my own thread. I can shear wool."

"Good to know. Come with me child. The stables are no place for pretty young girls like you to be wandering into. Besides, looks like you're a distraction to my stable boy," she added, whispering to me as she led me away. I didn't have time to say goodbye to Jonathan, but I gave a little wave of my hand from behind my back as I peeked over my shoulder. He waved back. I wondered if I'd see him again.

She pulled me into her gypsy tent and sat down uncomfortably.

"Is it hard to be pregnant and surrounded by all this – this circus wildness?" I questioned her.

"I am used to it. There are far worse things and far worse places I could be in. Besides, this is no ordinary child I carry. She is special. I suspect she will go far in this world, but I don't have money to raise her."

"I can help you raise some money," I blurted.

"And how do you propose that?"

"I'm not sure. But we will think of something. That way you can keep your baby."

"Who said anything to the contrary?"

I realized I had spoken too soon. I knew of Lily's fate, but Belladonna didn't.

"Oh, I just meant that –…"

Seamus came into the tent.

"Seamus, my beloved. What news do you bring?"

"It is not good news. I can't keep going into hiding Bella. Eventually they will find me, and kill me, and if I am seen with you, they will kill you too. There is a hefty bounty on my head. It would take a king's ransom to get me out of this alive. I must hide you or not be seen near you. I couldn't risk anything happening to our – our little flower." He placed his hand over her belly.

"Who? Who are you referring to Seamus?"

"The Boys."

"Who are the Boys?" I questioned. Seamus hadn't really noticed me before.

Gunshots fired outside of the tent and we peeked out. "Those are 'The Boys' – baddest lot of outlaws and criminals you ever did see gather. They're after our horses as payment for my outstanding debts. The house proprietors obtained a court order to seize them and everything. Bella, we don't stand a chance. I have no choice but to fight them."

"Fight them? You will do nothing of the sort Seamus McGee." She put her hands on her pregnant hips.

"I will take them away from here so you are not hurt. Maybe I can reason with them, but probably not. They have weapons where their brains should be."

"No, Seamus!" Belladonna pleaded with him. "You can't. You can't fight. What if something happens to you? I cannot raise this child alone! I cannot go back to my old ways. Lest I corrupt an innocent's eyes too soon and may the curse of the universe be brought upon me. A brothel is no place for a child!"

He held her shoulders to calm her down. She looked him in the eyes and melted. "Nothing's gonna happen to me, Bella. I just have to settle a few debts is all. You don't want to lose your horses, do you?"

Her eyes held hurt in them. "No of course not, but I don't want to lose you either." She kissed him through subtle tears. "I can't bear to witness you upon the gallows."

Seamus paused. "I'm not going to be hung. We're going to dead man's row – I've been asked to draw. I do not want you to follow," Seamus insisted.

"You will have no choice," Bella insisted.

"Bella, I beg of you. You must not follow. I cannot risk anything happening to you, or – or our baby." He put her hands to her belly. "Call her Lily. She's a little tigerlily, I can tell. Feisty, just like her mother, and just as beautiful."

Belladonna smiled, her nerves coursing through her. "I shall," she whispered softly through choked tears.

"You shall soon see, we will be victorious in this outcry of justice. I will set them straight. I will return soon and we can celebrate, my Bella." He kissed her goodbye and slipped the bullets into the empty slots of the gun barrel and left. She turned to me with tears in her eyes.

"Elisabeth. Go. Spy on my husband. Tell me of his fate. Carry this charm with you and I pray it brings you both luck." She placed a small stone in my palm. It had runes on it. I nodded and left.

Dead man's row was an alley between two back buildings. Seamus had been asked to a draw.

Standing before Seamus in the alley was a young man, no more than eighteen years old. He wore a sombrero hat with a wide green decorative band. His front teeth were prominent, as were his piercing blue eyes. He almost seemed likeable.

"Seamus McGee. I believe in giving a man a fighting chance, so we're's a gonna play a game of Russian Roulette." The man at the other end of the alley voided his gun of bullets except for one. He slid in the single bullet and snapped the barrel into place and spun it.

"Wee. Just like a game, idn't it?"

Seamus' hands trembled. He did the same.

"Want me to make 'im dance, boss?" one of the other 'Boys' shouted.

"Nah. I only need one shot. I only need one bullet. You see, this here gun has never let me down. I'm gonna kill a man for every year of my life and you're next. Number eighteen, Seamus McGee."

Seamus looked at the young man with fear in his eyes. Legend of him traveled throughout the land and his cunning, sharp shooting skills made him one of the most feared outlaws of his time.

Seamus was cornered. Even if he missed, one of the other 'Boys' would certainly take him down. I watched his fate unpeel before my eyes and it was very difficult to watch. This was checkmate for Seamus. He had nowhere to run or hide, but in order to protect Bella and their baby, he had to be killed. They would keep hunting him down, and the possibilities of Bella being injured were greater. Seamus had no choice but to surrender to the bandits collecting on their bounty.

He spun the barrel of his gun and laughed wildly.

Seamus dropped his gun to the ground and fell to his knees.

Like a coward, I couldn't watch. I looked away. How would I tell Belladonna of his fate? He was moments away from death. I couldn't bear to watch. I thought of Ethan.

The gun went off. I jumped with a startle and felt my heart stop briefly. I felt it. It was as though the gun had hit my chest and not Seamus. But it hadn't. There was silence. The only sounds were of maniacal laughter. I couldn't look to see if Seamus lay there on the ground, as I knew he must. I ran. I ran in the opposite direction. I leaned my back up against the side of an inn and caught my breath. He died on purpose! He knew what he was doing. He died to save Bella, and their unborn baby. This baby would be special. Somehow I felt it in my soul.

My words echoed throughout my mind. *Ethan, please don't die.*

Something ticked inside the pocket of my dress. I reached inside to pull out the pocketwatch. Without hesitation, I opened it, knowing it was a key to the portal. Not knowing where I'd land, I closed my eyes. On cue, Henry the owl hooted three times, and the portal was opened. *Hoot. Hoot. Hoooooooot.*

Chapter 8

THE BIRTH OF A STAR

he stood before me but did not speak. "Abigail?" She only stared out the window of the treehouse blankly, as though she had eyes. A draft blew cool wind across her face and her hair whispered softly as it swept.

"Abigail? I'm back."

I sat up. I had been lying down next to Ethan. I called her name again. "Abigail. Please talk to me."

She turned to me. "It is difficult."

"What is?"

"To see what you see."

I paused. "W-What do you mean?" The words came tumbling out of my lips carelessly before it clicked. Abigail saw Seamus die.

"I – I had not seen before. Even as Belladonna, I waited inside. I waited inside for your return. To tell me of Seamus' fate," she said with a sullen heart.

"But – but didn't I come back?"

"No."

"How come?"

She didn't say anything, but stared as blankly as her expression.

"Abigail, I – I don't know what to say. That must've been hard on you, I mean Belladonna, I mean-," I kept sputtering with self-consciousness and concern.

"It was harder than you think. But I understand now why his death was necessary. He died to save us. He died to protect us and keep us safe. And as hard as it is to accept, it was only his body that died. His spirit lives on. As now, I saw through your eyes and saw his death happen just before me. Only his silver thread did not find the light. Murdered, he lay in the streets, looking helplessly around for guidance. It was an angel that responded."

"An angel? A real angel with wings?"

Abigail flashed her silver eyes at me. "Yes dear. A real angel. Wings are actually just beams of light with the ability to expand great distances. It appears to humankind as wings."

I looked to Ethan who lay sleeping peacefully in his coma. Not even the sound of our voices could stir him, but I desperately wanted to. I wanted him back. I wanted him to return and to be okay.

"Seamus had many angels watching over him that day. What Seamus didn't know or understand yet was just who he was, and the role he would play on the future of our destinies. For several days, Seamus wandered as a ghost. Unable to see the light, or any pathway home, he wandered confused, but not alone. Seamus met up with an extraordinary being on his third day. This being changed him. This being appeared to Seamus as a great lion and attacked him. As the lion raged, Seamus found himself fighting back, but helplessly could not fight the tremendous beast. The soul of the great lion entered into Seamus and took him over, consuming him. The lion turned to stare at a woman. It was Bella. Belladonna stumbled upon Seamus at this very incident. The horror of seeing her dead husband being attacked sent her into madness. She tried to attack the great beast herself. She climbed aboard its back and rode it. As it took flight, she looked to the East and saw a new star. The star shot across the sky and upon it she made a wish. It was in her madness that she sought to seek revenge on those who had killed her husband. She cast a curse out into the universe, that her children would avenge his death, even if it meant their own deaths. They would be his crusaders. However, Belladonna did not know that she carried twins. Two children were born. One was Lily, as you have met already. The other was Rowen."

"Rowen? Rowen is your – I mean, Belladonna's daughter too?"

She nodded. "But not all tales have a happy ending. Rowen was born, but she did not live soon after. It was in her death that Belladonna took her to a nearby tree and buried her infant body. The tree grows close to here, and you've already seen its heights, but you must also visit its roots. It is in death that rebirth happens. Rowen is a dryad. She is a spirit that inhabits a tree, or anything made out of the tree, such as paper, or – a book."

A light went on in my mind's eye. "A book? *The* book? The book of the seven sisters? That's Rowen?"

She nodded and smiled. "She is the scribe, as she is also the book the words belong to. The pages are her skin, the words are her soul. She bares all for us, and thereby is the most vulnerable of us all. It took me a long time to find her again after she was stolen."

"Stolen?"

"Ahh yes. Would you like to rest first? Or shall I just send you back now?"

I looked at Abigail knowing I was about to feel the sands of time, once again, shift beneath my feet. "One request?"

Abigail smiled.

"May I take him with me?" I wrapped my arm around Ethan's chest and hugged him.

She smiled as I heard the owl. By the third hoot, I had awoken.

I lay nestled atop a boy, in a pile of hay. I had brought Ethan back with me. But as my eyes adjusted, I realized it was not Ethan, but Jonathan.

Our shoes were off and flung on the straw floor of the stables. My blouse had been loosened. Apparently, Jonathan and I knew each other very well. Our closeness surprised me in that even though it was Ethan's soul, I felt like I didn't really know this person.

"Is your arm, umm, hurting? I've been laying on it for awhile now," I asked, breaking into some conversation.

"Nah, it's fine." He pulled me back down into a spoon's embrace. I smiled.

"Thanks for spending the day with me," I said, pining for more information.

Jonathan sat up and kissed me. His kiss felt identical to Ethan! *But how?* "The pleasure of your company was all mine." He bit his lip and smiled. "You've charmed me, miss. I am under your spell."

I blushed. "I hadn't cast a spell on you, yet," I teased.

"Stay with me longer. Stay with me tonight. Just you, me, and the horses."

"What if Belladonna were to come here? She would probably fire you on the spot if she knew you were in here rolling around in the hay with me."

"Yes. Yes, she probably would," a voice came from the entrance of the stables.

Jonathan and I both looked surprised.

"Get dressed immediately," she ordered.

I looked down to my corset to see it had come loose. I shuffled to redress myself.

Belladonna looked at us with anger. She had a look in her eye of scorn and hatred, and heartbreak.

"But since I am fond of matters of the heart, I shall let you stay. You tend the horses well, and they all seem to be tamed by you. You speak to them in a way I cannot. Especially that one." She pointed to a black mare in one of the farther stables.

"Night Mare?"

"Yes. She is expecting a colt, is she not?"

"Yes Madame," he began and then corrected himself. "Yes M – ma – Belladonna," he stuttered.

"The colt is yours. Care for it as it were your own, as one day it will be old enough for you to ride it."

Jonathan seemed taken aback by her generous gesture. He doubted her.

"Yes. You are correct. There is a catch. I said the colt would be yours. But you must do something for me first. You see, this girl was supposed to report back to me news of my husband, important news. But she chose not to. Instead, she fled and I am only to find her here, in the arms of a stable boy!" I wasn't prepared to face her anger. Her eyes reminded me of Sadie's. *True love lost.*

"I can see you are mad," I started.

"Madness cannot begin to express how I feel. My truest love has been taken from me! Only his unborn child residing within me will remain here, walking the Earth with me, whilst he – he," she shed tears. Her heartbreak was felt by all of us.

"Stable boy. You are to take this peasant girl to the farthest tree you can find. Tie her to it, and leave her there. I wish for her to feel the pain of a broken heart as she watches her true love leave her behind in the distance."

Jonathan was speechless.

"I most certainly will not!"

"Then you both will leave my sight at once. I cannot bear to be reminded of your betrayal." As she commanded us, she grabbed her belly and almost fell over in pain. "Oh dear. It is time."

Belladonna had gone into labour.

Jonathan rushed to lay her on a patch of hay. "Get my father. He can help," Jonathan shouted at me. His father must've been a doctor. "Where is your father?"

"There is no time," Belladonna clutched to him. She lifted her skirt to see her water had broken. The imminent delivery was near.

"The inn. Go to him!" Jonathan shouted.

I ran outside and looked around. The inn wasn't far, but it wasn't near either. By the time I returned with Jonathan's father, it was too late.

Belladonna held two children in her arms. One of them didn't move. The other was a beautiful, dark haired baby girl. She was identical to the one that lay still. A stillborn.

"Oh Bella," my voice quivered as I spoke the words. I could not bear to feel the pain she felt. I watched her expression. She was in shock. Seamus was gone, and his only offspring lay in her arms. One of them had already rushed to be by his side in death. The littlest angel, Rowen.

She held up the baby to Jonathan. "Take her! Take her from me and bury her. Bury her far so that I may not feel her grief." Her sadness echoed through her voice. "Take her so that she may never feel mine."

She gazed upon Lily's eyes.

"Lily. I shall cherish you, for you are the one that remains. You are the one that will rise up the spirit of Seamus within you, so that he may live on. Lily, you are a gift from the Divine."

It was in those words I saw it. The light. The wings. They shimmered from Lily's tiny body and radiated around her. At her head was a crown. A halo of yellow light. Her aura could be seen easily."

Belladonna looked cautiously at Jonathan's father.

"We must hide you. For this is no ordinary you child you hold. This child will do wondrous things. This child is the grail."

Jonathan's father turned to the little baby Rowen. "And you too child, shall do great things, in the depths of the beyond. It is through your voice of wisdom that we shall hear you. And one day, you shall reunite with us and help us defeat this death which took you so hastily." Jonathan's father took the baby Rowen into his arms. "I shall make sure she is buried underneath a tree, so that, like a tiny acorn seed of a rowan tree, she will grow again."

Belladonna held tight to the baby Lily as the sound of a great bird echoed throughout the stables. A raven! It came swooping in through an open window and aimed itself directly at the infant.

"Bella! Shield the baby so the raven does not peck at its eyes!"

Bella did as she was told. "I am cursed! This has become a foul place of death! Those that I love are taken from me! Oh Seamus, it is in your memory that this little one will live on. But how – I have no means to pay for her upbringing."

The voice of a woman, familiar to me but not easily placed, came into the stables. It was the Queen of Sands, the Black Widow. The raven landed on her hand and she held it there perched as it looked at her with grim satisfaction.

"You are a fool, Bella! You will have no way to raise a child on your own! I... I can help you," she tempted her. Deceit was in her voice. I knew I was not allowed to mess with fate, but I couldn't help myself.

"Bella, don't! Don't listen to her! She's lying!" I yelled.

"The child! The child – she shimmers!" The Black Widow Queen observed. "She is the one!"

"No! You cannot have her!" Bella screamed.

Unbeknownst to me, fate never let anything stop it or get in its way. A portal opened and swallowed Bella. Before I could blink, I watched Bella get thrown through time. She was gone in a flash. I knew she had been thrown back several hundred years, to the 1600's. Lily's fate rested before me. I had to save her! I pushed the Black Widow Queen out of the way and grabbed Lily, swaddled in a piece of Belladonna's torn dress. Jonathan's father quickly observed that a distraction was necessary. He scooped up a pitchfork full of hay and tossed it on top of her, pinning her to the ground underneath its weight.

Jonathan's father tossed the stillborn baby into Jonathan's arms. "Take them. Take them far from here. Hide them, as many will seek them. Flee Jonathan! Flee while you still can!"

"Come on," Jonathan grabbed me around the waist and led me to the last door of the stable. Gypsy Epona was there. "It's Bella's horse. She'll take us wherever we need to go."

We both quickly and speedily mounted the horse and fled out of the stables. I wondered of the fate of Jonathan's father being left behind with the Black Widow Queen.

We sped on the horse. I did not know where we would wind up. Gypsy Epona rode for a long while, but finally settled upon a steady pace and we trusted she'd lead us to safety. It was midnight and the sky was clear. We followed the northern star and headed towards the east. It took a great effort for us to cross such a vast amount of land. But time didn't seem to matter or exist, as there was nothing around us in all directions. It appeared as desert would. I looked down at my arms and resting inside of them was an angel, shimmering just like a star. It was now my job to protect her.

Chapter 9

THE SHIMMER

onathan and I traveled for many days. I had never ridden horseback for so long before. It was exhausting. We stopped in many small towns, mostly to rob goats of their milk to feed Lily. We stole bits of bread and meat from drying racks. We went unseen. We took no more than we needed and trusted we'd be provided with anything else if the unexpected should decide to reveal itself to us. I knew the horse would lead us to our purpose. Finally, Gypsy Epona came upon a clearing and walked straight towards a tree. I knew the tree. It was Rowen's tree.

Gypsy Epona lay down at the base of the tree and let us dismount her. Carefully, I carried Lily in my own arms as if she were mine. Jonathan carried Rowen in his. Seeing the death of a child stirred him. I worried if he would recover.

"Why does there have to be so much hatred in the world?" he screamed into the air. "It's a child. Did you have to take a child?"

"Jonathan. Who do you scream at? God?"

"Yes. I don't know. It's just a child," he said flustered. He fell to his knees and sobbed, exhausted from the journey.

It's not as though my heart was made of stone, but knowing the fate of Rowen somehow made it easier to absorb her human death. I knew her spirit would live on and do great things. But it was hard to tell that to Jonathan.

"But we are blessed Jonathan. We are blessed with this new life and we shall raise her as if she were our very own."

Jonathan looked perplexed for a moment, but slowly absorbed the idea. He kissed the forehead of Rowen. "Let us lay this little one to rest."

"So that she may be reborn."

"Reborn?"

"Yes. Her spirit. Her spirit will not die, Jonathan. I believe it will transcend and transform into miraculous things. Just look at her sister. Can you not deny that she's nothing shy of an angel?"

"Well yes, she is sweet. All babies are sweet."

Jonathan could not see her wings, but I could. She shimmered. Suddenly I felt concerned that if I could see her, so would others. Those who would seek her out, to kill her, or worse.

Gypsy Epona neighed with worry. A swarm of black ravens headed for the limbs of the tree.

"Protect Lily," Jonathan shouted. "Cover her."

Gypsy Epona did something amazing. She grew wings! From out of her shoulders, Pegasus was born! Gypsy Epona took flight and flew all around the birds, using her wings like vast protective shields and ricocheting them off to the ground. It was similar to the spell Abigail had cast that night at school.

"Look there!" Jonathan pointed to the ground of the tree. It had opened. A hole had opened into the ground. A hole just large enough to fit a baby.

Without hesitation, Jonathan put the infant Rowen into the ground. He went to cover her with dirt, but the ground swallowed her instead and the hole closed up on its own. Jonathan took two steps backward in amazement and confusion at what had just happened. He turned to face the ravens, and to shield Lily.

"There are too many of them," he shouted, as scores of ravens attacked him and he fought them off. "I cannot hold them off for much longer."

Gypsy Epona spread her wings completely around the tree, forming a protective circle around it. Light shone from her wings so strongly that it bounced the ravens away. Flustered, they flew away. She fell to the ground, exhausted.

"Oh no. She is weak. We need to find food, and soon, before those birds come back."

"Did you see her wings Jonathan? Did you see them? That is no ordinary horse! That is an angel horse. That is Pegusus!"

"Don't be silly girl. It's just a horse."

"Jonathan! You cannot deny the mouth of the earth opening up and taking that dear life from your hands. You cannot deny it opened on its own and took it into the core of the tree. You saw it with your own eyes. I know you did!"

Jonathan didn't speak. He had seen it, but didn't want to admit he had.

"Elisabeth – I – I can't explain it."

"I can't either. But I trust in my heart that this horse, this magical horse, brought us here because it knew we would survive here.

Do you not believe in magic? Do you not believe in miracles? Are they not one in the same?"

"No of course not. Miracles happen at the hand of God; magic is – is witchcraft."

"You say that as though it is a bad thing!" I scolded him.

"It is! All magic is bad. Magic can lead to nothing good." Jonathan crossed his arms stubbornly in front of him. He was different from Ethan in many ways, but similar in several too.

"I don't believe that. I believe that magic is neither good nor bad, but it has potential to be either, depending on the source. Like fire, or water, it is an element. It can warm or it can burn, or bless, or drown."

"May your soul have mercy, Elisabeth. You speak as though you are one of them."

"One of whom?"

"Heretics. You know, the times of the Inquisition are not too far behind us. They like to burn witches, and drown them too."

"Yes. I believe that. I'll take my chances. I know better. I'd harm none unless they warranted it. I hold in my arms a blessed gift from the Heavens. I will devote my life to her protection, and strike down anything that stands in my way."

As I said those words, lightning struck the tree behind us. It severed down the center, just as it was the day I met Rowen, as an adult. From inside the tree, light shimmered.

I peeked my head inside to stare down into the core of the tree.

"Be ever cautious. Lightning may strike again, Elisabeth."

Softly, I said to Jonathan, "Look."

He peeked inside the core of the tree. Rowen lay swaddled softly inside, but she glowed with the charge of electricity. Jonathan attempted to reach inside to retrieve her, but when he touched her, his arm received an unexpected jolt and he jumped backwards.

Out of breath, he panted and looked befuddled.

He saw her.

Rowen had transformed.

Like a metamorphic butterfly, Rowen's swaddling clothes fell to the side of her and all that was left was a ball of yellowish crystal shimmering light. The shimmer.

Jonathan didn't say anything, but instead left his mouth open to spill the words unsaid and sing the songs unspoken. Jonathan's eyes told me that he acknowledged the magic before him, and the miraculous transformation of this blessed child.

"She shimmers! She is like a star fallen from the heavens. She is golden," Jonathan's eyes lit up with enthusiasm, and worry. He looked to me, and to Lily. "Lily will need to be protected."

"Yes."

"Your eyes, Elisabeth! Your eyes! They glow!"

I wasn't sure what happened. I felt compelled to offer Lily to the tree. I held her out from my arms and over the core of the tree, recently struck by lightning.

"Elisabeth! You must not do so! Lightning! It will strike again! I am sure of it!" Jonathan said panicked. A calm came over him. The eyes that I saw from were not my own. I recognized them. I saw through Abigail's eyes. This was a moment she needed. I realized it was I who needed to go back through time and rescue Lily from the Black Widow Queen; to rescue her from her current fate of the present. Abigail had presented me with a gift; a gift I must now accept, and challenge for the purpose of saving the fallen star, the littlest angel.

Just as the lion overtook Seamus, the light from inside the tree overtook Lily. Lily was bathed in a faint, blue light. It blended with the crystalline yellow light of her sister, Rowen. The two blending can only be described as the way the blue flame touches the bright yellow of a candle fire. It flickers. It dances. It melds together. The light shimmered, and then faded. The glowing light from inside the tree went missing.

Before us, the tiny infant body of Lily floated upwards and hovered above the base of the tree. The energy of the glowing yellow ball of light separated from tree and surrounded Lily. Rowen cradled her sister. Jonathan went to grab for her, but I held him back.

In a flash of light, Rowen and Lily shot up to the height of the tree and hovered at its crown. Together they glowed, the star and the angel, atop of the split tree, crowning it as though it were a Yule tree. Then they both shot up into the stars.

I looked to Jonathan confused. My eyes had returned to normal.

Lily and Rowen merged – the Gemini – the two became one, briefly.

"Look. Look here at what has fallen," Jonathan ran to the spot near the tree where we both saw the silver light. "It is – it is a ring."

"Jonathan, that is not just a ring," I said excited.

He held the ring sideways and circled it near my finger. "It is a promise, fallen from the stars. A circle that holds the star in its heart."

I slipped the ring over my finger and felt the familiar tingle. I knew it belonged to Lily.

At my feet, a book appeared. The book.

I bent to lift it, but did not open it yet. I simply stared at its cover. The familiarity of it beckoned to be opened, but I knew once it was, my journey would soon end. I'd met my challenge. It was I that needed to come here and do these tasks. It was I that would be the instructor for others.

I opened the book, knowing that Jonathan and Ethan were one and the same, and I would see him again. He was never far from me. He really was a soul mate, traveling through time with me. I looked into the center spiral of the portraits of the seven sisters. I felt myself being pulled through the book and out through the other side.

Chapter 10

AWAKENING

I lay with my arms around Ethan. I had the book in my hands. We had returned to the treehouse, only this time I looked at Abigail, she smiled.

I knew that my time travels had purpose, and many dangers I would have to face in them. I had seen beyond the fourth dimension. I had seen and felt and heard the realm of the angels. And it was my job to rewrite history and change the destiny of the fate of a glorious golden child.

"You have brought both Lily and Rowen back to me. But this ring – this ring you must give to me in our past. One is a key for the other. But of course you've figured that out. It is why you were able to find the room in the present. You had the ring. The ring is Lily, and she stays hidden inside, protected from harm. You also must place the book in the house that Emelia and Sadie grew up in. You will return to their time again soon, but you must leave it just as quickly, for you are in danger of slipping into time and getting lost in it, perhaps changing your own destiny forever, as well as the destiny of those around you. You must make haste and beware of the dangers. You have stirred the Black Widow from her grave. We mustn't disturb that which we have already rid our world of, or we risk an even greater battle than we possibly could ever imagine."

"How did I bring Rowen back?"

"Rowen lives in the book. She is the guardian of it. It is she who makes the words appear and disappear at will. If eyes fell upon the book and learned our secrets for the wrong reasons, we might all meet with grave misfortune. So the book is inhabited. Rowen is a dryad, a tree spirit. She can never take human form – at least not fully as you and I. She speaks through her words of wisdom."

"I knew that."

"Yes. I knew you did, dear. Just making sure you're paying attention. Sometimes the things of greatest importance are right before your very eyes and you will miss them because you're not paying attention. Such as love. You often miss it because you are looking too hard or not hard enough. I bet you wondered why Harding recognized you, didn't you?"

"Yes. How did you -?"

She smiled. "I know everything. Now off you go," Abigail waved her hand. I didn't even hear the owl, as I'd teleported too quickly. Abigail didn't use the stopwatch as the portal this time. She'd just sent me back.

Once again, I didn't have the stopwatch. But I clutched tightly to the book. The ring still encircled my finger.

"Good," I whispered under my breath. I needed to get inside unnoticed. I'd landed in the front yard, rather unpleasantly and near the spot Hremm Nevar flew down on me. I felt his presence among the woods and ran to the door.

I crept inside.

"Elisabeth?" George Finch peeked out of his study. He was a cute old man, with many mouse like qualities. I noticed he had a heavy amount of facial hair above his mouth, which he twirled at the ends. He also had a triangle patch of hair on his chin. He was rather a hearty fellow, with his shirt barely held together by the buttons pulling at the seams.

"Yes. I just took a walk." I kept the fancy and gilded book tucked underneath my arm. I hoped Mr. Finch would just think it was works of Shakespeare or the Bible and not ask about it.

"Fair enough. Have my daughters shown you to your room yet?"

"Oh yes. Yes, of course. I will show myself up, thank you."

And with that, I quietly crept up the familiar stairs that led up to Emelia's room, my room of the present.

"What are you doing?" Emelia peeked her head out of her bedroom.

"I thought I'd go up to bed. I feel very tired."

"Would you like some cookies? And milk?"

The thought of food sounded wonderful. But I couldn't just leave the book lying around. I had to get it to the secret room. "Umm, how about in a little bit?"

Emelia came over and snatched the book from my arm and placed it on the table that led upstairs. "Come. Let's go before they're all eaten by Sadie. She loves to steal them when they're fresh and leaves me with the broken ones and crumbs."

"But my book," I said, reaching my hand to the book as Emelia pulled my arm in the other direction.

"Your book will be fine. We're only going to the kitchen. Do you like shortbread?"

"Hmm? Oh, yes, of course," I said, feeling defeated and worried. I wasn't completely satisfied that the book was safe, but perhaps Emelia was correct. Who would want to steal the book anyway?

Sadie.

Nervously I accompanied Emelia to the kitchen and we retrieved fresh cookies. I attempted a move to leave the kitchen, but Emelia lingered.

"Isn't it beautiful?" she said, gazing out the window of the door that led to the back of the house.

I went to the window to look at what she saw. "Yes." My answer was short, but courteous. All of my focus was on the book. I'd worked so hard to get it and Abigail reminded me to make haste. Stargazing was not making haste.

I took a footstep to leave when Emelia grabbed my arm and then let go. "Wait, please. I need someone to talk to."

"About what?" I hoped this wouldn't take too long, or perhaps even a conversation that could be brought with us upstairs. I continued to try to nudge my way out of the kitchen.

"It's Harding."

I didn't feel as compelled to move. "Harding?"

"Yes. He's a very special boy. But today, he confused me. I found him with my sister, Sadie, down by the lake."

"Oh?" I played innocent and listened quietly. I had seen the whole spectacle, but Emelia didn't know that.

"And he was kissing her, and she lay there naked underneath him and he tried to convince me that she was drowning? How gullible does he think I am? Why should I believe him, or her? He confuses me so." She bit into her cookie.

I bit into my cookie also. I had no words. But I did know that whatever answer I gave her would affect her destiny. She was losing trust in Harding. I had nothing to gain by seeking Harding's affections in this life, as I wasn't from here. Harding belonged with Emelia. True love or not, they were meant to be together in this life.

"I think you should trust him. It is your sister that causes concern to me."

"Sadie?"

"Yes. I need to return upstairs. Please excuse me."

Anxious and feeling impolite, I ran back up the stairs. The book was still there, but it had been moved. I peeked to Sadie's door to see that it was cracked ajar, before it shut itself, probably at the hands of spying Sadie on the other side. An eye appeared in the keyhole and then left again. She had spied on us!

I snatched the book in hand.

"Elisabeth?"

"My apologies for my impoliteness. Thank you for your hospitality. I'm tired Emelia. I'll show myself upstairs to the attic." I pressed the panel underneath the table and entered the hidden stairwell.

Familiar as the room was, it still felt different being in the past. So much was so different. But I had to know for sure that the book would be safe. I walked to the cupboard and opened the door.

This time, it was not linens that existed inside. It was the secret room. I had found it again, in the past. I stepped inside with the book.

The secret room was the same in the past as it was in the present, for it existed between the worlds and time. As it was mentioned in the parchment left for me by a messenger of Rowen, …

> *This house harbours a secret book, in a place where time is both found and lost, in the heart and soul, where above and below are conjoined and all things within it are universal.*

It had no time. Still, this hadn't occurred to me when I'd left the door to the cupboard open in my haste to place the book inside. My existence within the secret room did not go unnoticed. I was discovered.

"What are you doing?" a voice said softly. Sadie stepped into view. "What is this place?"

"Sadie! You need to leave. You need to just go back out the same way you came in. Go now, before your mother misses you."

I held my hand over the top of the book – the book I'd worked so hard to retrieve. Sadie had not threatened me yet, but I knew what she was capable of. There were many steps still involved in defeating Hremm Nevar, and I felt it necessary for Sadie to continue in her present time.

"You're missing a few pages," she snickered as she held up torn pages from the book. She *had* stolen them! I flipped through the book quickly to see a chunk of pages gone. One page that was left looked to be the end of a spell – a lightning spell.

"Let's see who has the last laugh now Sadie Finch!" I pointed my finger at Sadie and flung her out of the room with the same technique I'd used to open and close Emelia's door. I had new powers in this time slip. I wasn't about to let them go to waste.

"What have you? What is this place? You're a witch! I'm telling mother about it!" Sadie protested. I pulled the door shut, but it had no lock.

Sadie, the ever thieving rogue. Would she open the door? Could she? I wondered if it would open again from the other side, but it did not reopen.

Abigail. Yes, go tell her!

I considered what to do next. I knew the book would have all the answers to all the questions I sought that existed only in the universe. They had to be retrieved. I would need to remember what Abigail had said about the book.

I looked above me, but the infamous constellation of the seven sisters was nowhere in sight. Clouds covered the night sky. Frustrated, I opened the magical book. Before my eyes, text appeared. Text and drawings, magical spells, sigils and seals, pictures of constellations and directions within the stars. There it was! A star map. My eyes laid upon it and I knew I was home. But why did it seem so familiar? A vision of flying through the universe entered my mind, but quickly was lost.

I memorized the page and its position in the night sky, knowing that somehow it was reflected down here on Earth. Its presence was significant.

I blew dust from the page. My breath disturbed hidden ink within the page. Discovery! A new star map formed, only this one formed along the floor. *My breath has power?*

I looked around me and stars appeared on the floor, seven in total. At the heart was the pedestal with the book. At its base, a white star with seven points formed. It pulsated and drew a line radiating from one of its points to the stars. One of them glowed. I walked over to see which one it was. It must belong to me. I lifted my foot to step on the star, but was interrupted.

A wind swept through the room, disturbing the perpetual order of timelessness. Time shifted. A portal had opened. It was not Abigail that created it. It was the Black Widow, the Queen of Sands. Through time she'd traveled and found her way to the secret room. She was not alone. She had brought her minion, her raven, with her who most likely was a close relative of our well known Hremm Nevar.

"So you think you can fool me? I cannot easily be tricked. Where is the girl?" she shouted. "Where is the child? Send me back an imposter! Do you not think I can see the difference? You cannot hide her from me. I'll sniff her out."

I moved from my star on the floor and the star map disappeared. I moved back to the pedestal to guard it. I feared she would find Lily. I feared she would sense the ring on my finger and attempt to take it. I pulled at the ring to slip it off my finger, but it would not come off! I pulled harder, knowing if she did not see it, she would not know about it. It would not budge. Instead, it only glowed and glimmered, annoyingly untimely.

"What? What is this ring you wear? This band of silver? Or is it gold? It shimmers of a metal I've not seen before." She zeroed in on the ring with her eyes and I hid it behind my back.

"Let me see it!" she demanded. The book let off a twinkle.

"Oh? And what is this clever book about?" She approached it and ran her fingertips over the cover. I sensed immense danger from her being in the secret room. I wondered how I could summon Abigail, but she already existed in the current time I'd traveled back to. I knew there was only one thing I could do. I pushed her back through her own portal.

Unfortunately, she took the book with her.

Chapter 11

THE CALLING

he star map along the floor had disappeared, leaving no clues to what to do next or how to return to my own time. "This is bad!" I scolded myself aloud and paced the room.

There was a knock on the cupboard door as it opened.

Abigail.

I ran to her and threw my arms around her. "Look, I have to tell you something, but telling you might have serious consequences. I'm not sure what to do."

"What are you doing in this room? How did you get in here?" she seemed puzzled. "Where is this place?"

"You don't know?"

"Should I?" she looked around perplexed. As she walked, something changed about her. The closer she got to the pedestal, the more her appearance changed into the Abigail I knew of the present time, my current future. Finally she stood before the pedestal. She turned to look at me and her eyes were as white as her hair.

"Abigail?"

"Yes, Alyson, I am here."

"Alyson? You called me Alyson. But what time are we in?"

"You are back in the present, just as I, but only in this room."

"How did you open the door?"

"Sadie alerted me of its existence. Now my daughter has awareness of its location, which is not something she had previously. Time has been disturbed. This moment in time may alter the future as we know it. I kept the secret room hidden from Sadie all these years! Alyson, I fear we may have caused a butterfly effect. It is essential we go back to the present to see if the course of events is the same."

There was worry behind her blind eyes.

"Can't we just go back in time and erase it?"

"No. Sadie is a witch. Unlike Ethan, whose mortal life was easily spared as a gift by the Elders, Sadie's life cannot be tampered with. She can and will retain her powers and knowledge through time, life after life. There are some powers Sadie possesses that can be used against her own kind! Now that she's had access to the secret room, she may remember – oh my dear innocent Alyson, I fear the worst for my daughter."

"That is not all. In our efforts to save Lily from the Black Widow Queen, she now has kidnapped Rowen. Rowen is powerful, but defenseless. She is a book, and books have no power on their own, but words – words have power. She is only powerful by her information she might potentially reveal, and that is power enough. If the book stays in the hands of the Black Widow Queen, who knows who she might share the information with, including ... Hremm Nevar!"

My worry matched hers. I'd never seen Abigail so concerned and I knew that I might've potentially put us all in danger.

"You still wear the ring. The ring will lead you to the book."

"But how do we know which time it is in?"

"We don't," she began. "But the ring will. The ring will be your guide. Lily will help you find her sister. Bring her back to us as quickly as possible. And the Black Widow Queen has a name. Her name in the time you will meet her is Lucinda."

"Lucinda. The Black Widow Queen is Lucinda. But why is her name important?"

"Names have power. To call someone by their name is to summon them. Many of the dead are stirred this way."

A serious look washed over Abigail. She looked cold. "I must get back to my own time lest I get lost here. You will be fine. Remember what I have said."

I began to search my pockets for the pocket watch when Abigail interjected. "Oh, one more thing. Lucinda is staying at the house of her brother, the demon Magnamalphas. And I use the term 'house' very loosely. It is inside of a deep cavern. A cavern known as the Black Hollow. Do not stay for very long, if you can prevent it. The energy there is quite draining. You might even say, it steals the life right out of you."

With that, Abigail walked away and exited the cupboard back into the time of the past. I pondered on what she had just said. *A house of evil. Demons? And I have to go find a book inside of it. Why can't I just do homework and worry about chores like everybody else?*

I pulled out the pocket watch and opened it. It didn't tick. I was inside of a timeless room, a vortex, a portal between the realms. Sacred space. I knew I had to return here with the book. The vision of the star map was fresh in my mind's eye.

"Take me to Lucinda, Black Widow Queen, Widow of Death," I commanded of the pocket watch. I waited for the pull and out of the room I left uncertain of the time or place I would land. Where I landed was nothing short of Hell. *Am I dead?* I wondered.

To describe it would be like describing a place of death, covered in ash, the way the ash still rests around the ground of the dead trees surrounding a volcanic explosion. Nothing but death survived what appears to be an apocalyptic battleground. Bodies were scattered everywhere, some still aching to be put out of their misery. Storms brewed in the distance and scattered bursts of lightning scanned the ground searching for living trees to kill. This was a dryad's nightmare.

There was no house. There was a cave. A very black cave cut out from a large rock wall with shearing cliffs to either side of it. Bats continually flew in and out. A pair of jackals rushed towards me, but then stopped. Their eyes glowed red. Demonic dogs. I had reached the gates to a place I'd never want to be. They waited for their master. I covered my ears to shelter from their growls which pierced through my brain with a maddening reverberation.

My heart raced, but I had no time to panic. I had a mission to complete no matter how ugly it was presented to me. Rowen was in danger. I hoped the ring would offer some sort of shield or protection. I kissed it and approached the mouth of the cave.

A dank stench seeped out of the mouth. I covered my own mouth in attempts not to dry heave. Large rats and cockroaches ran over my feet in mass exodus from the cave. My heart skipped several beats. This would take more courage than I'd expected.

I stood before the massive cave. Several branches loomed above me. Familiar black ravens hovered watching my every move. They squawked louder. I stepped inside the cave. My footsteps were covered in a blanket of blackness. As I stepped deeper into the cavern, my feet descended into black, murky goo, resembling tar. Hearing the sounds of bats flying about the cave, I realized the substance was guano. Bat poop. Unfortunately, my hands skimming the walls so I would not fall also offered a similar slimy substance. I wanted to cry. *Why me?*

I had a backpack with me. I reached inside it to find a candle and some matches, but no flashlight. I wasn't sure what to expect if I lit the candle, but it had to help. I struck the match and licked the flame. A pair of eyes stared at me from the other side and then vanished.

Nervous, I dropped the candle and its flame extinguished. I crouched down and fumbled for the candle, feeling around the bat goo and dry heaving. I found the candle and relit it. Looking around, there was no one. But the cave went much deeper. Behind me, from outside of the cave, lightning continued to strike down trees randomly. I pressed on. I followed the opening of the cave, walking in the center and avoiding too much bat goo. The walls were painted with bloody handprints. I was not the first to be here. The handprints unsettled me, especially considering they faced the direction leading *out* of the cave, and not in. Who or what waited for me inside?

I turned the candle to come face to face with what appeared to be an undertaker. An incredibly grim old man with shallow skin and deep set eyes, his hand outstretched and gestured for me to follow him. The jackals escorted him and thankfully left me alone, for now. I wasn't even sure if he was dead or alive, but uncomfortably, I followed his outstretched bony finger leading me down the corridor to a doorway.

He stopped and turned to look at me as he pushed the door. His face showed no change of expression. "Umm, thank you. I'll show myself in."

The inside took my breath away. The air was rancid. A woman stood in the corner petting a raven perched on her hand.

"I've been expecting you, Alyson," she said. My heart stopped.

Chapter 12

THE RAVEN'S MISTAKE

couldn't believe my own ears. *She knows my name. She knows me.*

My instinct was to run, but I couldn't run. In fact, my feet couldn't move at all. The bat guano had solidified and I was held firmly in place by it. Death by bat poo. This is *not* how I envisioned I'd go out in this world.

"Thank you for inviting me into your home, *Lucinda*!" To prove she didn't have the upper hand on me, I called her by her own name also.

She took a step back and then grinned.

"You are wise. I was not expecting one so wise to be so young."

"Age is not an indicator of wisdom. A newborn baby has all the wisdom of the entire universe, but cannot communicate it yet," I spat defensively at her.

"A newborn baby you say? Did you come to tell me where the girl is?"

"What girl? Does she have a name?" I taunted her.

"Yes, of course she has a name, child." She softened up her voice, making my guard go up in her obvious deception to pry it from me. She didn't know Lily's name.

"Then what girl do you speak of?"

"THE CHILD!"

I shook my head and smiled.

Lucinda became furious. Her true colours reminded me of the tantrum of the fake Princess Lily back on the day of the RenFest.

"You would be wise not to meddle with me! I can release one thousand deaths upon you; deaths you've only dreamed of in your worst nightmares. Your life is in my hands," she said and let out a cackle. There was no doubt she was a witch also, but not on the same side of things as me.

"I am not here to meddle with you."

"Then why are you here?" she asked. The book was not in sight. I wasn't sure what to tell her. My legs began to feel heavy and weak.

I changed the subject. "Who are those lost souls outside?"

She laughed. "They've come willingly, just as you have. They just chose not to leave, comforted by me and fearing the final death I will give them is far worse than any physical death they would feel. The death of your soul hurts much, much worse." She grinned.

Pain seeped up my legs. I had to move them. I shook them in attempts to break the shackles of the bat goo off my feet. A small piece chipped off and then another.

"It is pointless to try to escape. I said you came willingly. I did not say I would let you leave!" she scolded. Frantic, I stomped my feet free of the goo. Something glimmered from the corner of my eye. It was the invisibility cloak! I grabbed it and wrapped it around me.

"YOU CANNOT HIDE FROM ME, YOU CLEVER GIRL!" she shouted. Her eyes darted into another chamber. Panic swept through me. "MAGNAMALPHAS!"

"Yes, my Queen?" a deep, hoarse voice thundered through the cave. It took my every ounce of being to keep still and not faint from weakness.

Magnamalphas was black as darkness could ever be, without becoming a shadow. His skin was a dark grayish colour, tough, leather-like, and rotting – exposing a shadow beneath the flesh in places it had been ripped off. His walk was unnatural. He walked on hooves. Scanning upwards revealed his thick arms and bulky hands, each with a fingertip which ended in a talon. I almost looked at his face, but closed my eyes. I sensed a black skeleton with no apparent flesh covering it, as though his face had been ripped off his ominous gray body. At his crown resided two horns, one for each side of his skull. I opened my eyes but did not look at him directly. Just his presence in the room left me weak and my stomach churned with the stench from his rotting flesh.

"Set this room ablaze so that she who hides behind the cloak will burn!" she demanded.

Magnamalphas accepted her command. He did not speak any words, but instead walked to a stone wall and swept it aside as though it weighed nothing. The stone wall flung through the air and smashed against an adjacent wall. A low growl followed by a high pitched hiss came from inside the wall. I could not look inside to see what made the noise. Whatever it was, it was very large. Fear ran through me.

He waved his skeletal hand and I heard the metal from a cage roll back, unlocking whatever was being held behind it. I watched as one curled razor-sharp talon came into view, followed by another and then several more until the body of it came into view. It was at least two stories tall! From all directions it blew fire from one of his seven heads.

Lucinda continued to cackle as she herself became surrounded by flames, but she was invulnerable to them.

It was a hydra! I thought they were only mythical beasts, but here before me was a two-story tall, icy-blue coloured, seven-headed hydra! Abigail hadn't warned me of a hydra. I hid along a crevice in the wall just beyond the lick of the flames.

My knees shook. I felt the blood inside of me turn ice cold and the pain of being drained was antagonizing. "Lily, I need your help. I need you to help me, please," I whispered to the ring.

There was an explosion at the mouth of the cave. It was Belladonna's horse, Gypsy Epona. She was flew towards me as another mythical creature, Pegasus!

The horse flew directly at the blue hydra and struck it down with a sonic wave pulsating from the enormous flapping of its giant wings. The hydra lay on the floor immobilized, but only momentarily before it regained strength. It blew flames at the flying horse. They were in heated battle. Magnamalphas fired balls of black shadow at the winged horse, but she dodged them, upsetting him further. I knew I had the distraction needed to flee my crevice and retrieve the book, but I'd have to hurry.

"Thank you, Lily. Please help me find Rowen."

I held out my finger with the ring and it pointed. I followed in the direction of the ring. A hand wrapped itself around my outstretched finger.

"I shall break it off! This ring! This ring is no ordinary ring! I sense magic here!" Lucinda held her grip tight around my finger, bending it in all directions making me wince with pain. The ring slid off and rolled to the ground, making a *ping* sound several times as it bounced along the stone floor. I kicked her and clung tight to the cloak, running in the opposite direction. I worried the sound of my panting breath would reveal my location, as well as the winged horse being able to withstand the heat of the blue hydra. It would take a great force to strike him down.

"Rowen," I called out. "Rowen, reveal yourself! I'm here to rescue you!" I shouted.

Lucinda's raven squawked as its birdcage began to rumble and shake violently.

"Nevar! NOOO!" Lucinda screamed at it.

Nevar? Was this Hremm Nevar or one of his offspring?

There was no time to think. Abigail had instructed me to make haste and I desperately needed to. I felt myself being drained of my very life essence every moment I stayed inside the Black Hollow. I felt the raven getting stronger. The seven-headed blue hydra shifted all of its attention on me. He lunged and flames shot out from his nostrils and mouth to an uncomfortable closeness to my own body that I pressed myself firmly up against the wall.

"That's it! Feed from her life soul, my pretty," Lucinda encouraged the raven perched in his cage. "Find her and feed from her. She is young. She has vibrancy. Feed from her and give it to meeeee!" her voice squealed. "I want her youth. I will consume her. She will be in me and I shall snatch her from this world she knows. That's it. Feed from her." Her fingers coiled around her hands. She had snakes for hair, snapping in all directions. Their unnatural hisses made my ears want to bleed. It was followed by a high pitched shrill of a woman screaming. It was the same banshee's cry Sadie had made to call upon her army of undead. I fell to the ground.

My eyesight went black and then clear again. I struggled to pull myself back up using a nearby chair made from human bones. I nearly fainted from weakness.

From underneath its birdcage was a slotted drawer. I staggered to it and pulled it open. The book lay resting inside. I reached in and grabbed it, fighting off the pecking bird with my arm. The cloak fell and my location was revealed.

"Not so fast!" Lucinda barked. Her hand gripped tightly around my wrist. It burned. A familiar pulse entered my bloodstream. I had been splattered with her own blood the day she was killed, the day Seamus attacked her and sent her spilling to the ground. I knew she would still be defeated.

She ripped the book from my hands and threw me across the room into a wall. It oozed. I landed flat on the floor. Weakness set in even further. Lucinda laughed.

She stroked the cover of the book. "All will be mine. All will be revealed, and you will be dead. But I shall spare you your last breath and let you keep that one. You will always keep your last breath, but it will be your only breath left. Everything this is yours shall be mine! And it's all here within this book. Let's just have a look, shall we?"

"No!" I exclaimed, riddled with weakness overcoming my body. Dizzily I attempted to stand to my feet, but with difficultly. I staggered and leaned against a wall for support as I watched. Lucinda opened the cover of the book. I feared Rowen would accidentally reveal her secrets.

"What's this? How can this be?"

She appeared furious.

"Only blank pages?! No, no, there is magic here. You can't hide from me! Reveal yourself!" she shouted at the book. "Yes! Yes! That is it! Reveal yourself. I shall possess the wisdom of the Queens of the Elders! And I will defeat you with it!"

If my breath could cleanse, I imagined my spit to be venom. A snake to a snake. Poison to poison. I spat at her. My spit burned her and she rubbed at her face trying to get it off as though it were acid. "Taste your own death!" I shouted at her. She dropped the book and I promptly grabbed it.

Gypsy Epona struck another sonic wave to the blue hydra and sent him to the floor. Magmamalphas growled. I averted looking into his eyes. I feared I might die instantly if I did. Several heads of the blue hydra snapped at us as I attempted to stand. I faintly ran to Epona and climbed aboard her back, with the book in hand.

"How did you –? You will not defeat me!" Lucinda shouted and shook her fist. As we flew off, I heard her laughing. The sound of it made me very uncomfortable.

Without prompt, Gypsy Epona flew out of the room and out of the cave, bypassing any ground or walls and shooting straight up into the Heavens.

"I already did defeat you Lucinda," I said to myself shamelessly. I held the book in my arms. Rowen was safe. "There, now both sisters—," my voice cut off when I looked down to my hand. My ring was gone!

"LILY!" I shouted back towards the cave, but it was already out of sight.

Chapter 13

A FALSE CALM

The horse continued to fly without any concern or distress about leaving Lily behind.

"Stop!" I commanded the horse, but she flew on. "Stop. Please! We can't leave Lily behind. We have to go back," I pleaded. Perhaps she didn't understand, or perhaps she did and was being commanded by someone else to come home. Either way, the flying horse was in charge and I had to comply.

Gypsy Epona flew around the stars. We zoomed past them with extraordinary speed, but still I held on with no fear of falling off. Oddly enough, it felt as though we were riding inside of a six-sided star shaped bubble of glass, but there was none. I was unsure why I was able to breathe normally, considering I flew around the universe. From the corners of my eyes, we passed through several familiar constellations. Gypsy flew around the belt of Orion and through the nebula. There it was, clear as a black chess piece of a knight, the Horsehead Nebula. I thought of Prince Ivan, and of Lily, left behind.

We flew up through Gemini and around through Taurus, and at its farthest end were the Pleiades. Beyond the Pleiades was a star familiar to our Sun of Earth. Gypsy Epona flew near it and flew towards a small silvery blue planet. When she flew through the clouds, the atmosphere was so similar to Earth that I gasped.

"It is alright," a voice said as we continued to descend. "Every human gasps upon their first breath."

"Who said that?" I looked around, with interest that this time it might be the horse speaking to me. "Gypsy Epona? Is that you?"

"No, silly. You will know me when you see me," the voice continued. It came from all directions. "You are now in my realm, the realm of the angels and the realm of the Elders. I shall explain everything once you land."

We entered through a gate guarded by a giant leopard crouched upon a rock. It shimmered with a yellowish-white auric light as we passed. It did not move from its position of guardian, but allowed us to pass freely. I sensed its leopard spots were only a guise for someone more magnificent.

Gypsy Epona settled upon a grassy place, filled with flowers and meadows and streams. It was breathtakingly beautiful. And the air was indescribable. It was the freshest, cleanest air I'd ever known. Every individual flower's scent made itself known and distinguishable. I could detect every audible animal's song and locate it as though they sang unified. The colours were so vivid, they looked to be painted. I wondered how a place so similar to our Earth could exist elsewhere in the universe. *Is this heaven?* I wondered.

But there were also noticeable differences. Sets of bizarre animals with two heads and flying wings traveled around us. Other winged horses flew overhead. This must be where Epona was born.

The sky was in a state of perpetual sunrise or sunset, I could not tell which. A sun and a moon were both present above me. A butterfly landed on my shoulder. I looked closely at it. It had a tiny head with facial features similar to a human! She smiled before flying off back into the meadows.

I looked around to see other humans, dressed in white linen robes. Many were barefoot. I attempted to listen to their conversation, but it was a language I did not understand. It had a melodic tone and almost sounded like a song when they spoke. If these were other human beings, they seemed to be highly evolved.

From out of the woods walked Sadie and Emelia, as well as Abigail. Abigail spoke. "We are all here. We have been waiting for the arrival of our final sisters. You do not have to hide here. This is your home, Rowen."

The book opened and the portrait of Rowen came into clear view. She had appeared. With a snap, she stepped outside of the portrait and stood among us. She was Lily's exact twin, except Rowen had dark skin. I realized she grew bark to protect herself.

"But wait, where is Lily? Alyson, do you not have the ring?"

I lowered my head ashamed of leaving Lily behind. "It was an accident. I tried to get Epona to turn back but she wouldn't listen to me."

"It will be necessary for us to rescue her, but for now, I sense she is safe. She has not been discovered yet."

"Abigail, you didn't warn me of the blue hydra."

"The blue hydra. I was hoping it did not exist. But you say it does. The seven headed blue hydra is a great threat to us, for it possesses an ability equivalent to each of us, including one head with my ability to heal. It will be a difficult beast to defeat and one best to be avoided if possible. No matter. It is only a beast. We have our own beasts we can call upon for aid. We also have powers to manipulate time and space, and the energies within. The time is now for you to focus not on what you are leaving behind, but on what you will be gaining in the future. The past and future have come to present and we all stand here in this grove. We are all the daughters of someone much more powerful than us combined, but, together we can band our energies into one and collectively defeat even our greatest enemies," Abigail led us in discussion.

"You sisters have been in the Black Hollow. You have felt the power and wrath of Lucinda, have you not?"

She continued. "And you. You have battled with Magnamalphas himself. There is no greater evil, and combined with the power of his sister, Lucinda, they are a tremendous force, a beast mightier than 10,000 lions and deadlier than 10,000 snakes."

"Why does she live with her brother, Magnamalphas?"

"Because once upon a time, she was a murderous woman, scornful and full of resentment for what man had done to her. She was filled with love and beauty, but betrayal took over her heart and turned it cold. She vowed to marry, to love as hard as she could and then on their anniversary of their first year of marriage, she would avenge mankind. She went through 365 husbands, killed one for every day of the year. Hence, she was known as the Black Widow. She knows of love, but has forgotten."

Abigail let out a deep sigh.

"Her son," she began, "was born of incest; a brother and sister so filled with lust and hatred. Magnamalphas took advantage of his sister in the worst possible way and she became pregnant. But that child was no ordinary child, being born from a demon father. Lucinda was filled with madness, but he threatened to kill her if she did not fulfill the prophecy and let the child be born. And so he was. Her son is Hremm Nevar!"

"Hremm Nevar?!" I said with a gasp.

"How dare you speak that name in this holy place!" Sadie yelled at her mother. "Do not bring up such a memory. My heart cannot bear it."

"Sadie, this is no time for you to retain all of your spitefulness. Remember who you once were. Just because you've descended and seen the realm of demons, does not mean that you become one yourself. You have fallen, but you have risen. You have a choice. You are a bearer of light, a keeper of a dark flame that has been rekindled anew into brightness."

"She is right, my sister," Emelia said to comfort Sadie.

"You have loved Hremm Nevar. You have loved the son of Magnamalphas and Lucinda, the King and Queen of Death. They know little of love and were ill prepared for the consequences of their son falling in love, a son of Death and born only to kill. You have shined a light into his black heart. Hremm Nevar is confused and gave you a black feather to call a truce when he could have killed you! It is because of you, Sadie, we will defeat Hremm Nevar and his ancestors once and for all! He had mercy on you because you were not afraid of him. You were not afraid of death. Because you had no fear, he had no power over you. You're free, Sadie!" Abigail cheered. Sadie fell to her knees and cried.

"But he still tempts me so," she confessed.

"Sadie, you are the only one of us that cannot feel the effects of the Black Hollow because you have the ability to become undead. That is an amazing talent. You can travel to the underworld and bring back knowledge so that we can eradicate death, we can defeat Hremm Nevar and the great Beast himself, Magnamalphas!"

Sadie gasped.

"Sadie, I fear this task may be too great for you to do alone, for it might certainly end badly if your heart gets in the way. Unfortunately, because of who you are, you cannot turn off your love like a switch. You will always be tempted by Hremm Nevar and therefore it will ultimately be your decision to kill him. You are his bride."

"Is there no other way, Mother?" Sadie pleaded to Abigail.

"I am not aware of one yet. But I do not risk losing you either. There is one who must join us to make the final decision."

Abigail held her hands out into a flower and blew them like a trumpet.

Flying in through the clouds above us flew in a great golden lion with wings. It was Seamus! His spirit lived on. Riding on his back, Prince Ivan as a valiant knight clenched tightly to the lion's mane. The great lion landed and Ivan dismounted. The lion changed into a man in linen robes and kissed Abigail's hand. He was no longer the outlaw I had seen of the late 1800's. He was a holy man and radiated light from within that could only be described as divine. I saw the recognition in Abigail's eyes. She truly loved him.

"My beloved," he greeted Abigail.

"Seamus, there must be a solution to this madness that our world has created. There must be a way to help them, those souls who still have no idea what's coming. A prophecy is only a prophecy. If we can prevent it, we will. But we need your help."

"It is Lily that will take my place on Earth now. She will be the one to do miraculous things. She is well aware of her gifts already. But she needs Alyson to guide her into the realm of the demons. Lily is an angel. She cannot descend willingly without losing her wings. It is through the appearance of a ring that she may travel. Once in the realm of the daemons, Lily must stay as a ring, but she can aid in the protection of Alyson. She can offer her a shield, a band of light that surrounds her. Auric healing and protection."

"So it is not Sadie who must fight, but Alyson?"

"Yes," he paused, "Alyson."

There was silence among us.

I had no words. I'd just been in the Black Hollow. I was not anxious to return. In fact, I'd hoped I'd never have to. But Lily had to be rescued. We could not leave her behind.

"Where is Lily?" Ivan questioned as he looked in all directions.

"Prince Ivan," Abigail began, "Lily is lost. Alyson rescued Rowen from the Black Hollow, but mistakenly, Lily was left behind. Lily will be fine so long as Lucinda does not wear the ring. If she does, Lily will have no choice but to protect her!"

"But the Black Widow Queen is dead. We've already killed her. I witnessed her death!" he rebutted. "I shall go into the Black Hollow myself and save Lily!"

"The present has been changed and the Black Widow Queen lives. Prince Ivan, you are forbidden from entering the Black Hollow as it is the Queen that created you, so can she destroy you. I'm afraid it is another one of us that must save Lily." She turned to me. "Alyson, I must warn you – you did not return to Earth for a reason dear. Earth is an apocalyptic battleground."

"What?" I let out a tiny gasp and could barely say the words.

"Your Earth is no longer what you'd expect to return to. Because Lily is with us, and also Rowen, time has altered. The stars have all been rearranged. You are now in the future of what has become the present. Many who could have been saved, chose not to be. Their souls were into the Black Hollow, where they will remain for all eternity. It is sad, but they knew love, they simply chose not to live in it. They could not see beyond themselves and therefore they perished."

"But Ethan!? And my father?"

"They are akin to us. Alyson, a soul never dies, only the body. You are never far from those you love and those who love you. Like an infant has an umbilical cord to its mother, so do we have a spiritual cord, a silver thread, to our mother... and father... as they are one. Ethan and your father are in limbo. They are not on Earth, but they cannot join you here unless you show them the way. Alyson, do you not know where you are? Of course you cannot – yet. You are in the land of the Elders. You are about three hundred light years from the present. Alyson, what lies below on Earth is the future. We need to go back and change it so that it does not happen this way. There are still many to be helped. Many to be healed. Remember, a prophecy is only that – a prophecy. And prophecies are not set in stone; they can be changed. We are seven for a reason. There are seven stars to which each of us is attuned to. We are, collectively, what humankind has been waiting for. Though we cannot save them from themselves – we can guide them, if they are willing to listen."

"Guide them where?" I asked.

"Guide them home," she answered. "Earth is not home. They need to look within themselves to find their true source. But for many, love is too powerful of an emotion, too painful to trust again after being hurt. Many have closed hearts. Unfortunately, you cannot change them. It is up to themselves to change. To see beyond the body that holds them. Therein a universe lies within."

I paused to speak, but no words came out. She must've heard my unanswered questions in my mind, as she continued.

"Trust that you will have all the answers you need when the time is right for you. There is one that must be defeated – one that still plagues the hearts of many – Hremm Nevar. If you can overcome him, you will have ultimate power to defeat the demon Magmamalphas and his Queen, Lucinda."

"How come she does not die? I have seen her die."

"Only her body dies, but it is her son who keeps feeding her souls to renew herself. She is as eternal as the Queen of the Elders herself, our Queen. They balance each other. You cannot have good without evil, black without white. There must be balance. I do not know of a way to completely obliterate Lucinda, at least not yet."

I swallowed deeply. I recalled defending myself from Lucinda with my spit. It became venom mixed with her death. I knew the only way to help those I knew down on Earth would be to descend into the depths of the Black Hollow and defeat the trinity of the Beast myself: Magnamalphas, Lucinda and Hremm Nevar.

"Alyson, prepare for battle," Seamus instructed and released his wings fully spread out to each side of him. He let out a mighty roar as he changed in a blink from man to lion. He was majestic to look upon. I had never seen anything so beautiful and radiant. "It is time to rescue Lily. My daughter's fate resides within you."

Chapter 14

WITCHBLADE

'd only visited the land of the Elders briefly, and I was enormously grateful for the privilege. But I knew it came with great responsibility. This was no ordinary place. I was not anxious to leave it, but knew that I must. I braced myself for what was to come.

"I'm afraid getting into the Black Hollow isn't quite so easy as just going back the way we came. One must be invited in," Abigail told us in detail. "There is only one of you that Hremm Nevar will invite."

"If Alyson is going, I'm going too," Sadie stood forward.

"If Sadie goes, I am going," Emelia stood next to her sister. They smiled at each other. Their sisterly bond of friendship had been restored.

"It will take the power of Pegasus to shield off the great blue hydra, so I too must go." My mother stepped forward and put her arms around me.

"Then if one goes, we all must go."

"Rowen crackled her barkskin."

"Do not be afraid Rowen. We will keep you safe."

"She is made of wood. She fears the flames," Seamus noted. "Rowen must be left behind, as must you stay with her, Abigail. The Black Hollow is no place you should be near. Abigail, I won't let you."

"They are my daughters! And Lucinda is no match for me."

"No, but for the very same reason you could not enter the lair of Hremm Nevar, you cannot enter the Black Hollow. You cannot harm, you can only heal. Even in your best attempts to defend yourself, you will die healing them. I cannot see that happen. My eyes, nor my heart, could not bear the loss of you, Abigail."

Tears fell down Abigail's cheeks. "Seamus, it is difficult to let my children go and defend themselves without me."

"Abigail, you musssst trusssst, remember?"

Abigail paused, and then smiled. She nodded. "It is sometimes hard to listen to my own advice."

My heart filled with hope.

"Alyson, I have faith in you. Be swift in your decisions, but wise. Choose your footsteps carefully as you descend into the Black Hollow. Get Lily back as quickly as you can dear, and when you do, use her as a shield. She can protect you, but you must make haste."

Why anyone would willingly go back into the Black Hollow was beyond me. It had plenty of dangers to face, and doing them alone made me all the more apprehensive. But it was something I had to do. Lily needed me. I'd already gone through time to rescue Rowen. I didn't want to lose Lily in the process. I wasn't totally alone – Gypsy Epona would be with me in full form. She was glorious as Pegasus. I didn't know I could believe in something so mythical and magical, but anything is possible in this world.

"I am ready," I said.

Epona stood next to me, ready to take me back into the atmosphere and descend down into wherever the Black Hollow existed. To find it again would be like finding a black hole. If we stay too long, we'll be lost forever.

"Take this," Abigail said as she handed me a dagger with a curvy blade. "It's a kris. You already know how to use it."

The blade had thirteen undulations. I took the cranked wooden hilt into my hand and felt its power. It was familiar to me. I had owned it before. I recognized it as the dagger I pulled from my garter before I met Belladonna. I'd killed a man with this blade.

"This is no ordinary dagger. Long ago, it was given to you, but you do not remember yet. It will come to you. Everything, in its own time, will come to you," Seamus followed through with Abigail's comment. To hear Seamus speak as a magnificent lion echoed deep within me. Seamus had a spiritual connection to us. I felt completely safe around him. "And you will know how to use it when the time is right."

"Contrary to what you're thinking, it's not for killing," Abigail added. "This dagger has a spirit within. All krisses have good and bad spirits, and in order to work properly, the kris must find the owner and be in harmony with each other. There are very specific ways to determine whether the spirit that resides in the blade is matched with you. One is by reading the markings left behind by rubbing it against a leaf. Another is by sleeping with the kris under your pillow. If any nightmares ensue, the blade is considered an ill fit, however good dreams mean good fortune."

Seamus continued. "It is an enormous vessel of power for such a small blade. Your blade will kill the mortal, but this blade also has powers over the immortal. It is a demon dagger, a witchblade. The blade will rattle in its sheath to warn you of danger."

"It will rattle in its sheath? It will rattle? It's alive?"

"Essentially. You will understand in time. It is also poisonous. A deadly toxin has been forged within its metal. This toxin is lethal to demons. There is nothing further I can tell you. You now have the information you need to go into the Black Hollow. Leave at once." He roared. "My daughter's life depends on you, Alyson. We all depend on you. Let our energy and prayers guide you."

Gypsy Epona knelt briefly so I could mount her between her enormous wings. With a wave of Abigail's hand, she was off, bursting through the open mouth of the outdoor gardens in the Land of the Elders. Out of the clouds and into the stars she flew. Once again, I had no breath.

A dark river in the stars led us to where to find the Black Hollow. Nebulas of black horses, night mares, made sounds of thunder as we flew past them. I felt my stomach go into a pit as she dove deep into an area of blackness. Surrounding stars were being eaten by this black hole, fueling it. My body shook with nerves as we plummeted faster.

I clutched the dagger as we flew back into the cave.

Immediately, the return of the sulfuric smell made me want to gag. We flew over the scores upon scores of wailing bodies looking for release from their perpetual torment. They grabbed at the hooves of Epona. She galloped on through the air and flew through the door that led directly into the chambers of Lucinda and her brother, Magnamalphas. They were not surprised to see us return, and unfortunately had set a trap for us.

Minions tossed a heavy iron chain around Epona's neck. She thrashed it back and forth, attempting to release herself from it, but they only pulled it tighter. They swarmed around her and pulled me off her back, tossing me into a cage.

"Welcome home," Lucinda greeted me. "I knew you'd be back." She approached the cage and ran her fingers along the bars, checking the lock with her long fingernail and grinning.

Gypsy Epona riled up and clawed her front hooves at the air. The minions pulled her to the floor with heavy chains and whipped her. I looked away, in shame and unaware of how to help. This was my mother they tormented.

Lucinda brought the cage holding the young Hremm Nevar closer to me.

"There now. Watch as she grows weaker and you, my son, will grow stronger. She has an amazing life force! Steal it! Take it, she is yours!"

The young Hremm Nevar squawked in his cage and flapped his wings loudly. As his wings flapped, my ears ached with pain. I collapsed briefly, catching myself on one of the metal bars.

Helpless, I clutched to the bars to stand and watched on as the minions carried on their torment, not just to Epona, but to several other victims they'd chained to the walls. Drained and weak, the Black Hollow took over me. Soon I would be lost.

I collapsed to the floor of the cage.

"Why not just kill her," I heard a voice say. I blinked my eyes and tried to focus, but could not. Everything was blurry.

"You cannot kill her. But you can drain her of any powers she has left!" The voice was Lucinda's. I blinked again and looked towards the cage of the young Hremm Nevar. I couldn't believe my own eyes. It was him! He was not just a tiny bird any longer. Hremm Nevar stood next to Lucinda, robed in his dark wings and his eyes black like coal.

"Leave her for now. I am well enough to feed. Let her recharge and I shall drain her once more upon my return," Hremm Nevar spoke to Lucinda. He then transformed into a raven and flew out of the cave.

I could barely lift my head. Lucinda looked at me and mocked my pain.

"If only you'd let me kill you, your pain would be gone," she scorned. "I can ease your suffering. But then, why would I?" She laughed and walked away into a deeper section of the cave.

I didn't feel whole anymore. Hremm Nevar had taken a large part of me, including my recently discovered powers. Still, there had to be something I could do to free myself.

I looked to Epona. She didn't move, but she breathed. She hadn't been killed yet either.

Sitting on top of a table, surrounded in a glass box, was the ring that held Lily.

A tiny voice from the bottom of the cage spoke up. "Don't say anything. Abby sent me here," a little mouse spoke. It was George! He was alive! "I came to get the ring, but couldn't lift the glass box. I think it is protected by a magic spell. I can't get Lily out! And now, now you're in a mess. You have to leave immediately!"

"But George, how did you –?" I couldn't finish my sentence. George had already leapt down and scurried across the floor to one of the hooded minion henchmen, who had fallen asleep sitting propped against a door. The keys to the cages and shackles were suspended from his belt.

"Oh George, be careful," I cheered him on in a quiet manner.

George quietly ran up the pant leg of the guard. The minion had a pig-like face. It was horrendous to look at. I stared at his closed eyes and watched ... and waited, as George unhooked the keychain. *Clink, Clink*. The keys hit the stone floor and made an awful sound. The guard's eyes opened.

Chapter 15

A CIRCLE OF PROTECTION

eorge looked petrified in the glare of the pig-faced henchman. He pretended to be just an ordinary mouse, perhaps one caught to feed the raven, but the henchman did not believe his own nose. He smelled George and growled. He chased George all through the cave and out of it.

The keys lay sitting on the floor.

If only...

I felt my heart sink. *How?*

I knew I had powers. I only had to discover them, and find out what was left that Hremm Nevar hadn't taken.

I concentrated on the keys. *Maybe I can move them to me with my mind?* Nothing happened. I squinted, as though it helped with my concentration, but still nothing happened. The keys remained sitting on the floor.

George ran back into the cave.

"Whisper," he shouted into the air. He appeared to be calling someone. "Whisper!" he called again. "Alyson, help!"

"What?" I couldn't understand him. *Call Whisper?* "Who is Whisper?"

"Elluna's wisp!" he shouted back and ran back out of the cave, followed by a very angry henchman. "Call to her now! You know how, just trust yourself!"

Whisper? What is a wisp?

I opened my mouth to call out the word Whisper, but instead a loud call, resembling a song, escaped. Within moments, a spiraling, blue ball of light entered through the Black Hollow and straight to my cage. I looked to the keys and pointed. The wisp spiraled through the air over to the keys and lifted them with invisible fingers. The keys landed at my feet.

"Thank you," I said surprised. A wisp. A ball of energy, and I controlled it. A connection was made between Whisper and myself as she danced around me and encircled me with her blue energy. I didn't feel just as myself any longer. I felt stronger. I knew I had the courage to break free.

I cranked my wrist to the outside of the cage well enough to fiddle with the huge iron key and crank it into the keyhole. *Click.* The cage door swung open. I was free, but there was a problem. Lucinda had returned.

"Well well, aren't we the wise one?" she called to me, noticing my wisp.

"Lucinda!" I barked at her, making sure to step out of the cage. She stalked me like prey, with her eyes. With a blink, she stood right before me.

She didn't say anything to me. She only stared into my eyes, as though searching for something. "You don't know who you are yet, do you child?" she taunted.

I didn't say anything. Just because I hadn't figured everything out yet didn't mean she had to know about it.

"I have one of the seven daughters of the Elluna right before me in this cage, and she doesn't even know it yet."

Elluna?

"Well I suppose now you're here to collect your ring, aren't you? Very well, be my guest. Who needs a ring, when my son already has half your powers!" She laughed, and her laugh echoed throughout the cave as though it were a huge and deep canyon. It shook my core.

She waved her hand over the glass box and it lifted. The ring lay inside on top of a beige, silk pillow.

"Go ahead. Take the ring," she encouraged.

I moved my hand in the direction of the ring, but hesitated. It was a trap.

"Take the ring," she growled.

When I resisted, she grabbed my arm and forced it in the direction of the ring. I sensed this ring was an imposter. This ring had no energy of Lily, or me, or Ethan residing with it. I thought of the kris, and the spirit within, and how if the two weren't harmonized with the wielder, the bad spirit would take over. This was Lucinda's trap. To take over what powers I had left.

I grabbed her arm and flung her across the room towards the direction of the cage. She lunged at me. I did not suspect she'd be taken down easily. George ran back into the room, followed by the henchman. The heavy footsteps of the henchman shook the room. The chiming of bells filled the room. I looked to the direction of the glass box. The ring fell from the box and rolled across the floor towards us. We both noticed the ring.

Lucinda and I gripped each other's arm and wrestled. Whisper flew wildly around us, launching herself at Lucinda. Lucinda winced with each shock of Whisper's sparks. Lucinda looked angrily upon Whisper. Her blue light sparked and frizzed. Lucinda tried to gain control of the wisp.

George ran over Lucinda's feet, breaking her concentration. I looked at Whisper. She had helped me already. I sensed she would help me again in the future, but only if she lived to survive the present. I nodded and she fled the Black Hollow. George scurried away unnoticed and hid.

The ring lay just at my feet. Lucinda noticed the ring and smiled. I didn't trust her to just grab it and put it on. It was enchanted. Enchanted with a demonic energy.

I pushed Lucinda into the cage and slammed the door on her, slapping the lock shut and caging her. Lucinda went into a fury. She sputtered unintelligible words, perhaps forming a spell. I had to hurry.

The dagger began to rattle. I pulled the kris out, gripped it with both hands on the hilt and slammed the blade into the center of the ring. Lucinda looked on.

"Nooooo!" she screamed at me.

The ring leaked blood on the outside. I quickly picked up the ring out of the blood and wrapped it in cloth to clean it. I held it up in front of Lucinda. Lily was free of her demonic possession of the ring. Lily's energy radiated from the ring. I slid it onto my finger and felt a circle of protection be cast all around me.

Magnamalphas returned to the cave. He was massive. His hoofed feet held up massive amounts of muscle, of a unnatural flesh colour – dark, rotting grey. Lurking behind his shadowy, skeletal face, his empty eyes flashed at me. I dared not look into them directly. Uncoiling his fisted hand, he held out his palm and it glowed with a red ball of energy hovering above it. He launched the energy ball at me.

Lily's shield cast around me and deflected it.

Magnamalphas looked angrier and cast another fireball. This time, I moved so it would be deflected towards the cage. There was fear in Lucinda's eyes as her brother's fireball hit her and she fell to the bottom of the cage. Distracted, Magnamalphas ran to his sister. I ran to Epona.

I bent down to stroke my hand along her fur. She sat up. I unlocked the chain that harnessed her and she stood tall.

"Are you sure you feel up to flying out of here?" I asked her.

She nodded and whinnied.

Magnamalphas threw fireballs at us, but the shield had now been extended around Epona too. His fireballs only ricocheted back at him, making him dodge each one with a growl.

"George, come on! Run!"

The little mouse ran hurriedly towards Epona. Magnamalphas's blue hydra lifted his foot and stomped it. He missed!

I gasped and covered my mouth. Whisper flew towards him and grabbed the tiny mouse. She lifted him and deposited him in my palms. George tucked himself into a pocket. I briefly caught a glimmer of a tiny faery inside the wisp. She was too quick to confirm. She fled the cave. We were soon to follow. Haste was of the essence.

The blue hydra's tail pounded at the floor as Epona rushed over him one last time and flew up out of the cave. Flames shot out from the mouth of the cave at us, but we had fled.

Lily safely rested around my finger as we flew back to the Land of the Elders. Magnamalphas, Lucinda and Hremm Nevar all still posed threats to us. It was Hremm Nevar! Hremm Nevar stole my powers and I wanted them back!

Chapter 16

THE **RETURN**

lluna stepped out before me. She was my mirror, only older. I could not tell her exact age. Her skin glowed a radiant white from within, exuding a halo of illumination all around her. She wore a crown of what appeared to me as little stars, encircling her but never touching one another. Her gown was indigo blue, the colour of the night sky and like Abigail, her hair was white. Although it was not the white that came from hair turning at old age, it was a luminous white, a colour unable to be duplicated in any salon. It was a colour graced by iridescent moonlight.

"Three hundred light years?"

"Yes, three hundred light years in the future, but I also exist in the now."

Whisper flew to her and danced around her before landing in the palm of her hand. When she stopped dancing, her blue light faded. I looked closely at her. She was as tiny as a faery, no larger than four inches tall.

"Well, you are no bigger than a hummingbird?" I said to Whisper. She smiled, laid down on her stomach in Elluna's palm and propped up her head. She flashed her wings at me and a blue light faintly shimmered up their edge. She twinkled. I looked to Elluna. "And so, I become you?"

"You already are me, a shard of me," she said with a smile. "You are one of my daughters. Let me explain it simply. As with any gem, it is first found anew, and very rough around the edges. Over time, waves and sand wash over it and make it smooth, and polished. With every life, you become more polished, shall we say. Until one day you become enlightened and achieve placement amongst the ascended masters, such as myself. I am a Queen, but I am not alone. I too have sisters and brothers akin to myself. It was my voice you heard when you first entered the gates to our realm aboard Epona. She received instruction from me to bring you here."

"How old are you?"

"I was born on the eternal day of the eternal month of the eternal year. The time created on Earth was created by humans, not by the Elders. We are ageless, as you are also. You will see. There are still some tasks you must carry out on Earth before you can continue further on your journey. You must defeat Hremm Nevar and his parents. It will be a difficult task. I have faith that you won't let us down. Still, it is unfortunate, but I must send you back down to Earth. There are people there that need you, and you have a life to carry out. Just because you know where you will end up, doesn't mean that you will get here on your own if you do nothing to assist. There are rules you must follow. Follow them and I shall see you back here. If you do not succeed, it will be the end for us both – but you will succeed."

She continued. "It is alright. I understand that it is difficult to comprehend anything outside of the world you know as Earth. But Earth is just a planet. There are hundreds of planets across this vast universe, and many fascinating places that you have yet to discover. This is only one of them. I brought you here because it resembles your Earth and makes you feel at home."

"This must be heaven. It is paradise. I don't know how else to describe it. Waterfalls, and lush meadows, and ponds. It's so beautiful!"

"My child, you have not died. I am permitting you to visit as I need your help. This – this is the land of the Elders. You have reached the Ice Castle, which is the heart of our world. I shall change it again to what is normal for us, but it may appear strange to you." The scenery changed as though it had been painted away.

It was unlike anything I'd ever seen, but enormously beautiful. I was surrounded by clear quartz-like crystals resembling frozen icicles, but they were neither cool nor hot to the touch. They felt like ordinary stones, but with a charge in them. Occasionally they changed colours. Elluna stood by something I could only explain as a pipe organ, a huge pipe organ. She pulled from it a purple crystal and a sound was made audibly that I could not duplicate using any human made instrument, other than perhaps a tuning fork. The sound resonated in my heart. I felt complete peace within as though I'd been filled with pure love.

"You see, in our world, we all speak the same language. It is music, harmonious with one another. There is no anger here, or fighting, or the hate that exists in your world. That is man-made. Humankind has a choice to live in peace, but they choose not to. They choose to live in fear of one another. They do not listen. It is for this reason they will perish, and not just their physical forms – their bodies, but their spirit will cease to move on. Nothing in nature chooses a parasite over a paradise. They will not be saved. Our planet can mimic many forms, including your Earth. Yet our atmosphere is different in that we do not age here, nor experience death. We live eternal. We have no need for the desires of mortals, such as your cars or money. As you can see, we exist quite simply. We can create our own destiny."

The scenery changed again. This time, I stood in an apocalyptic battlefield. Everything around me smoldered and smelled of burning plastic.

"This is what will happen to your world. It is not only war that causes destruction, but other abuses of power and hatred amongst your people. It is unfortunate, but humankind has been warned and chooses not to listen. They do not help one another as they should. Some do, but it needs to be universal. Humankind behaves like rebellious orphaned children, lost and spoiled with their own egotistic desires. They wander aimlessly, without purpose, waiting for instruction or someone else to save them when they should listen to their own intuition, help one another and help themselves. It is only when a catastrophic event occurs that they choose to bond and assist one another."

"I don't like this world. Can it be stopped?"

The scenery changed back to the room of crystals. "Yes, of course. There are many on your planet who are listening. They hear us. We whisper into their hearts, just as I whisper to you now. Just imagine what your world would be if everyone knew of love and peace. You can help teach them. It is actually very simple. Small acts can have great consequences. You will take this knowledge back with you. You are reborn from this day forward. You have witnessed the eclipse. You cannot go back, for you cannot unlearn knowledge. It is within you, as it always has been since the day of your birth. Use it wisely."

Whisper attempted to speak to me, but I did not understand her. She flew over to me and kissed my cheek. It felt like a butterfly kiss. She flew back to Elluna's palm.

"There will come a day when you will understand. You will speak all languages for all languages will become one. And the language you learn will not be of words. Words are often harsh when spoken. Nature is not made of words. There is communication in touch, gestures and sound. A rolling creek would not sound the same if it gave any other noise."

The sound of a rolling creek entered my ears. Immediately my mind transported me to the kissing bridge over Hollow Creek. I smiled when I thought of Ethan.

"I must return you to your own home, for there is much work to be done to repair and prevent any further damage. You won't remember much, but you will have glimpses. And I shall give you hints and reminders. From now on, every time you are visited from a spirit, you will find a white feather and you will know that we are near. You will find a way to get your powers back. You already know Hremm Nevar's weakness and with what to defeat him."

"Sadie."

"Yes," Elluna agreed with me. "He denies that he loves her, but already she has entered his heart and he cannot control it. It is she that can teach him love, something foreign to him. Love is a greater power than hatred. Teach love. It is easily learned, but takes greater effort to keep. It only takes one person to change the world, for the power exists within you. You will see."

I wished she could just give me all the answers right there. To tell me what to do, what moves to make and what my next step would be. But I guess no one really knows that, and even if she could tell me, it would take all the fun out of adventuring.

"Abigail, my daughter," Elluna greeted her. Abigail kissed Elluna's hands.

Abigail approached me. "I am thankful to see the return of Lily from the Black Hollow." She placed her healing hands on me, and also on Epona. "You have done well and shown us your dedication to fight to rid the world of the death and decay that has overcome humankind. You now know what is necessary to find your path to your destiny. We cannot show you, for it is something you need to find yourself. But as Elluna has said, we can give you clues to let you know we are near."

I picked a flower from the ground and another quickly grew in its place.

"There is no death here, only rebirth. This knowledge is already stored in your mind. You only have to unlock it if you have the right key." Elluna reached out and touched my forehead. There was a kinship, a bond, of my eternal soul as she resides within Elluna.

Abigail and Elluna smiled.

"We shall see you again soon."

There was a flash and I opened my eyes to find myself on the floor of the treehouse. I had awoken, but was I asleep?

Chapter 17

THE ANGEL IN THE TREE

y memories of the Black Hollow had already faded. I looked to the dream catcher hanging in the window. There was something so ordinary about the dream catcher. I knew in my heart I had visited beyond what lies on the mortal realm. I had walked through the dream catcher and experienced very real dreams. But were they only dreams? It felt like I'd just woken from a very bad nightmare, but one where hope lied at the end. *Was it just a dream?*

I stood up and walked around the treehouse. This time, Abigail wasn't there. It was only Ethan and myself. Was it just a dream? Did I fall asleep with Ethan? I ran to his side and nudged him.

"Ethan? Ethan, wake up."

"Huh? Wha?"

"Ethan! You're alive!"

"Of course I'm alive. You okay, Alyson? What time is it?"

I couldn't find the stopwatch. "I'm not sure."

"We'd better get back. Grams' will wonder where I've been. Come on, Shadow."

From out of a dark corner leapt a little puppy.

"Shadow? Where did you come from? I left you at Grams' house after the accident." I was bewildered.

Ethan hadn't heard me as he peeked out the window. "Whoa. Looks like more freezing rain is on its way. We'd better be careful. I'll go down first so you can hand me Shadow."

Déjà vu. I'd lived this moment before. Ethan's accident hadn't happened yet.

"Ethan, no. I don't think we should risk it. Let's stay up here until the storm passes."

"But Alyson. Grams' will worry."

"Grams will worry more if something happens to you."

"Nothing's going to happen to me, Alyson. I'll be fine."

"No, Ethan."

Ethan stopped.

"No. Please. My intuition is telling me we need to stay right here."

"Okay. Okay, you've convinced me. I don't like the look on your face. You're scared. It'll be alright. We're in shelter up here."

I wanted to cry. I wanted to thank Abigail. Ethan had a second chance, and I did too.

I rushed to put my arms around Ethan. "I love you," I said.

Ethan seemed taken aback. "I love you too, Alyson."

The moment went completely serious. Second chance or not, I knew Ethan was the one I wanted to be with, forever. I'd held him in past lives, and let him go. I'd lost him to others. Abigail had shown me that.

"Ethan, keep me warm."

"Come on. Lay back down." Ethan wrapped the sleeping bag blanket around us. "Want me to tell you a story?"

I nodded. Anything to distract me from the ice outside. Shadow groaned. Ethan patted the edge of the sleeping bag for him to lay down.

"When I was younger, I used to come here a lot. It was a public park, but not too many other people knew about it or came here. It was quiet for the most part. But I always wondered what it would be like to have a girl up here with me, and now I know." He smiled.

"What did you fantasize about?"

He laughed. "Oh no. I'm not sharing everything. But you're much more interesting than any fantasy. Anyways, I also liked to come here because of my telescope. It's been busted for awhile now. Grandpa gave it to me. He's probably responsible for why I like looking out into space so much. Have you ever wondered what's out there? You know… if we're alone in this great big universe?"

A glimmer of my recent travels passed through my mind but quickly was lost.

"I have. I guess we'll just have to wait and see."

Chapter 18

A HAUNTING RESEMBLANCE

chool was back in session…

The school library was often my refuge. I found solace in being alone among the stacks of bookshelves filled with dusty treasures. I heard them. The words – so anxious to be read. Each book called to me. But there was only one book that concerned me now. The book in the secret room. My book. Rowen's book. The book of the sacred seven sisters.

A white feather flew into an open window and landed on the desk right in front of me. I picked it up and stared at it, and then my eyes darted over to the barely open slit of a window. *How did that?...* I looked down at desk I'd fallen asleep at. I still had my pen in hand, resting calmly over the notebook I'd taken many notes over in class, as well as written many love notes to Ethan from. Ethan had been on my mind all day. It was apparent his soul and mine were connected somehow.

I looked to the notebook, and to the page I'd left it open to. Names had appeared, as well as a date. I'd scribed something curious. I looked at the names, and picked up the white feather.

Curious.

The room with the microfiche machines was always quiet. Hardly anyone ever used them anymore. I went to the card catalogue; an old-fashioned, but useful tool. There had to be something I could use. I scanned the names and useful books on genealogy. I found one for the year 1887.

It took me a few moments to locate the reel of microfilm holding the text. I wheeled it onto the machine and lined up the ribbon. Adjusted vertical, then horizontal, okay, perfect. The pages whizzed by until I slowed them down. Watching them pass made time seem cleverly distorted. Page after page they reeled. Until it stopped. I didn't stop the machine. It did. And there it was.

A portrait. A charcoal sketched portrait of Elisabeth and Jonathan Tarlington. I threw myself back from the chair and looked on in amazement. It was real! I had existed before. The resemblance to me now and me then was uncanny. The sketch easily could be Ethan and me, but the clothes were so old. I was a gypsy, and he, a stable boy.

I read the article below the picture. It haunted me, but I yearned to learn more. I wasn't sure knowing this information was particular helpful to my own sanity, but it did pique my curiousity into the world beyond, and the world before. A bell rang.

It is now I know who I am.

ELISABETH AND JONATHAN TARLINGTON. WANTED FOR MURDER AND PILFERING HORSES, AND WITCHCRAFT. A BOUNTY FOR THEIR HEADS $180 EACH.

I sat silent and just stared at the screen. *We were wanted criminals?* Nervously I turned the forward dial. I watched the pages whizz, and they stopped again. There before me was the same image! I scrolled the pages forward. The same image on each page! The portrait of Elisabeth and Jonathan. Before I knew it, the pages scrolled themselves. And the portraits began – to move.

As though I watched an old tin-type movie in slow motion, Elisabeth and Jonathan played out a story before my eyes. Elisabeth motioned for me to come closer. I moved in closer to the screen of the machine, a bit reluctantly. I wasn't sure I trusted myself from the past. Elisabeth spoke to me.

"Alyson, you must listen to me. To learn the fate of yourself from a past life, is both a blessing and a curse. If you are certain you want the knowledge, I will show you what happened to us. You only have one chance to make this decision. You cannot go back and unlearn once I have shown you. Choose wisely."

I was curious, but also, I didn't want to know. I doubted I could bear to see myself, even from a past life, die. I knew Elisabeth was right. I knew I was right too.

I shook my head. "I don't want to know."

"As you wish," she said.

The microfilm burst into flames setting off the sprinkler system. Spouts from the ceiling rained on me like some indoor shower. In a moment, I was soaked through and the librarian had rushed into the room. Off in the distance, fire truck sirens whirled through the air.

"Great," I said, self-loathing in my decision. I'd hoped it was the right one after all. *I guess I'll never know.*

I was wrong. That night brought with it an unexpected turn of events, a conversation with Emily. And a yearning to know answers and more about myself – or rather, the history of my soul. My soul's journey. *Where have I been? Who have I been? ... Who will I become?* Everyone is always talking about past lives, but no one really reflects on our *future lives.* But now I do. Three hundred light years away exist answers held behind lock and key until the correct time. It's a door I'm anxious to open, and if I had to pick the lock, I would.

A mass clump of grey fur purred quietly at the foot of my bed.

"Emily?"

"Yes, Alyson?"

"How did you react when you learned of Harding's death?"

"How did *you* react when you learned of Harding's death?" she said, but smiling.

I cocked my head curious at her. "What do you mean?"

"I saw you. I remember you. These memories weren't there before, but they are now. How did you end up in the past?" she asked.

"I'm not sure. Abigail, I think. She sent me on some tasks."

"Harding had an interest in you, didn't he? Oh, Abigail is so wise."

"Emily, I'm not sure. He belonged with you back then. I only went back to do those tasks Abigail wanted me to."

"The point I'm making, is that your Ethan, might someday remember his past lives too."

I paused to reflect. What if he did?

The phone rang.

I flew out of bed to answer it before the rest of the house woke up.

"Hello?"

"Alyson?"

It was Ethan. Emily's ears perked up.

"Hey, what are you doing up?" My voice sounded nervous.

"I don't know. Can't fall asleep."

"Oh?"

"Yeah." There was a long pause. "I'm coming over."

Click.

"Ethan?"

I looked quizzically at Emily. She sat up and changed into the girl, Emelia.

"Alyson, there's something I haven't told you."

"What? What is it?"

"Do you remember the first time I took you through Sadie's scrying mirror and into the land of dreams?"

"Yes, of course."

"I wasn't completely honest with you then. You see, Harding's soul, Ethan's soul, is bound to us – all of us sisters. He will fight to defend any of us. Also, Harding has a true love, as you may have guessed – it's you."

"But then why would you say he was your true love?"

"I loved him, and he loved me, yes. But the moment he met you, he changed. A new soul entered him, the soul of your Ethan. He loved us both. I did not tell you, as watching Harding that day in the mirror with Hremm Nevar would affect you greatly. You weren't ready as you are now. You are stronger and wiser. There is nothing more terrible, than witnessing the death of someone you love, especially your soul mate. It is perhaps why Abigail chose to save Ethan from a similar fate as his former life as Harding. To die so young, it was tragic. Abigail knows all too well about losing the one you love. It is perhaps why she couldn't bear to watch you go through it again."

My mouth was agape. I did not know what to say.

"I know it may take awhile to understand, but you will. There is also something else troubling me," she began, but was cut off when we heard the rattling of the lattice against the side of the house.

Emelia glanced at the window. Ethan was there. Ethan's eyes looked directly at Emelia, the girl now, and not the cat. There was recognition in Ethan's eyes. He had seen her. Emelia quickly transformed back into a cat.

My window pane lifted up with the aid of Ethan's hand. He climbed in. "What was that? Alyson?"

"How – How did you get here so quickly?"

"I ran here. I had to see you. But wait – first tell me what I just saw, because I know I'm not going mad. There was a girl here. She was talking to you."

"This house is supposedly haunted, Ethan. Even Grams thinks so."

Ethan paused. "So. You're not denying there was a girl, here, sitting on the edge of your bed?"

I shook my head.

"Where did she go?"

I shrugged my shoulders. "Maybe you saw a ghost?" Emily purred on the bed beside Ethan. He looked down at her and then to me. I smiled, trying not to smirk. It was my little secret.

"This house is really weird," he said. An exuberant Shadow jumped up and licked Ethan's cheek. He gave him a noogie on the head.

"Yeah. Tell me about it."

I looked at Ethan, and saw Harding, and Jonathan. It was all the same soul. Amazing. I wanted to tell him, but waited.

"Alyson, I came over to tell you something."

"You didn't have to do that. You could've just told me over the phone."

He held something over my head. It was sprig of fresh mistletoe. He kissed me.

"I couldn't do that over the phone."

Something happened.

Our kiss had a connection much deeper than it ever had before. He threw me on the bed and kissed me for a solid hour after that. I heard the grandfather clock chime midnight.

"Ethan. Ethan, you have to go."

"Why? What happens at midnight? Do I turn into a pumpkin?"

"Cute, but no. No, I just don't want to get caught with you here. How would I explain how you got here?"

He smiled. "Alright."

Ethan opened the window and looked outside.

He rushed over to me again. His skin was cold as ice from being in the open window. I quickly warmed him. "Ethan. There's so much I want to do with you."

"Then why? Why are we waiting?"

Ethan's energy after an hour of kissing was like that of a bear. Fearless and full of testosterone, Ethan kissed me again without giving me time to think or answer. His power both excited me and scared me.

Panting heavily, I stopped him. "Why do we always stop? What are you afraid of?" Ethan asked, in an aggressive tone that confused me.

"I'm not afraid, Ethan. But just because you're ready, doesn't mean that I am."

Ethan hushed. I'd never felt so much power coming from Ethan. He radiated it. "How are we going to do this? How am I going to be next to you and not be tempted? I want you, Alyson."

Frustrated, he let out a huff. I debated what to do next. It would only take one time and it would be over in a matter of minutes. We'd have done it. And then what would happen? We'd just end up being one of those teenage couples I dreaded that had sex all the time because there was nothing left to look forward to. I didn't want that and something earnestly told me neither did Ethan.

"We made a promise, Ethan, in the treehouse. I want to keep that promise. I don't want to give into this feeling. We have a little more self-control and respect than that."

"I know."

There was a long pause.

"Ethan? Don't be mad."

"I'm not mad at you, I'm mad at myself. Here, I pride myself on being a gentleman and I'm not being very ... umm... gentlemanly."

"Maybe we're just taking things too fast?"

"Yeah. It's hard to know when to slow down." He pet Shadow on the head. Shadow rested his head on Ethan's knee.

"Someday, we can do all these things you dream about. I promise. You're worth waiting for," I said.

Ethan smiled and leaned over and kissed me softly. "You too."

He went to the window and opened the pane. A blast of cold air zipped through the room. "I'd better run home fast before Grams notices I'm gone." He blew a kiss and descended the lattice. I leaned out the window and watched his shadow run across the snow towards his house before closing it.

Emily changed back into herself. "You know, he loves you. It's why he can't control his emotions. Because he's been with you before. He knows on some level what he's missing. It's hard to have that level of intimacy at your age though. You're wise to know what you're getting into and to cool it down."

"But you – you're still a virgin. Do you feel like you're missing something?"

"No, not really. I've seen Sadie get herself into enough trouble for the both of us with her promiscuousness. Besides, I have far more important things to worry about. As I had started to tell you before Ethan came over, I am troubled by Sadie's latest behavior. She and Hremm Nevar are at a truce, but I've witnessed her sneaking outside again and venturing down towards the lake. I suspect she is having secret rendezvous with him."

"What does that mean? I thought she was mad at him."

"She was, but she loves him. That is what was troubling me before. You see, Sadie wants desperately to rejoin the light, but is lost in the power of the darkness. It easily consumes and absorbs her. It is only a matter of time before she is tempted by him again, and in darkness, she will be extinguished, like a candle flame being snuffed out. Left in darkness. I know my sister. She craves power. Add to that she can already harness the power of lightning and she may be the most powerful witch of us all! She can defeat the darkness, but does she have the strength not to rejoin it?"

I saw the concern in Emelia's eyes. Without Sadie as our ally, Hremm Nevar would be as difficult to defeat as the day we trapped him in the mirror. There would have to be another way.

Chapter 19

THE MORNING AFTER

ilently, I crept up quietly to the attic and turned the corner. The cupboard door – was open. Towels and linens lay strewn about on the floor. I folded the towels back and placed them into the cupboard, closing the door behind me. I turned to walk away from it when I thought I heard music, similar to a high pitched bell, chiming from it. Looking back over my shoulder, the area around the door was outlined in a shining yellow light.

Not wanting to wake my parents or attract them to the cupboard door, I walked quickly back to it and placed my hand to the handle and pulled. The inside of the secret room was completely illuminated. I went inside and pulled the door behind me.

I looked up to the clouds in the sky through the observatory window in the ceiling. The sun shone on the floor and it was illuminated. Once again, I walked to the star map on the floor. As though I'd been invited, I stepped on a star. I closed my eyes and hoped I'd be able to accept whatever came next.

Light came from the book. The yellow light poured out from the open book on the pedestal. I walked to it and attempted to look inside. Its luminosity made it difficult to stare directly at the pages. I placed my hand on the book.

"Do you remember me?" the book asked.

"Yes, vaguely. I have only glimpses of the journeys that Abigail sent me through."

Rowen stepped out of the book. Her body was the shape of a glowing yellow energy. I couldn't decide what element she was other than spirit. She resembled water, but she was not wet. She resembled fire, but she was not hot. I reached my hand out to touch her.

"No. You must never try to touch my energy directly."

I pulled my hand back. "Okay."

"I had hoped you'd see me. There are few that can. What are you aware of?"

"What do you mean?"

"There are still chapters missing from the book – Sadie removed them. They are most likely near the lair of Hremm Nevar at the lake."

"But where should I look for them?"

"Pay attention and you will receive clues from the Elders. They are trying to help you regain what was once lost, rather stolen, from you." She began to fade. "I cannot stay out of the book for too long. Good to see you Alyson, my sister."

And with that, she shimmered back into the book.

The floor faded once again. I opened my eyes and looked around. The room was the same as it ever was, free of any tear or wear, or dust or anything that plagues ordinary rooms. But this was no ordinary room.

Uncertain what to do next, I stepped out from the cupboard. Something caught my attention across the room, in a mirror. There was a shoe underneath the bed. But it wasn't a tennis shoes or a flip flop or any modern day shoe. This shoe was old. I retrieved it from underneath the bed. It was a white leather lace up boot. It belonged to Elisabeth.

"Curious," I said softly.

A silk cloth peeked from inside the shoe. Metal peeked out from inside. I pulled it out carefully and unwrapped the silk cloth. There it was. The dagger – in the present day. I wasn't sure how it arrived here, if it had been placed by someone. Perhaps that's why the cupboard door was open. But who left it open?

I questioned if my mother had somehow discovered the secret room and just not told me. I had to find out. I ran down to the breakfast table to see her sipping coffee.

"Hello, sweetheart. How did you sleep?"

"Pretty good." I wondered if perhaps they'd heard Ethan climb up the lattice at midnight. She didn't comment. I moved on. "Mom? I was wondering," I began, but paused.

"What is it, dear?"

"Did you know we have a spare room in the attic?"

"You found out how to get into the attic? Oh, your father will be delighted. He's been asking me if I knew where the stairs were and I didn't know. How did you find it? Can you show me?"

"Sure, follow me."

I led her upstairs to the level of the bedrooms and to the mahogany table in the hallway. "It's just right through here."

"Where?"

"Here," I said, pressing on the wall and opening up the panel.

Mom had a look of surprise, and stepped inside. I followed her in.

"How could I not have known this was here?" she said.

"I only just found it a few days ago, and I assumed you knew about it already," I said, telling a little white lie.

"But this room – this room is wonderful and would make a good sewing room or art room. I mean, look at these paintings. They're beautiful." Mom was awestruck. I kept glancing at the cupboard. I knew in my heart she had a right to know. But maybe she had to discover it on her own. If I showed her, Abigail instructed it might have consequences. "Well, it's good to know this is up here. Thanks for showing it to me. I'm going to head back down now and get some things done."

"Welcome. I'll be down in a few. I like the view from up here."

With that, Mom descended the stairs and I stayed behind. It was a curious bedroom, with odd angles and no doors other than the one at the base of the stairwell around the corner. I sat on the bed and reached my hand underneath the pillow. My hand slipped over the silk scarf and pulled out the dagger.

"I don't know what this means, or why I'm supposed to have this now, but I'll keep it safe."

I decided to take the boot and the dagger downstairs with me to Emelia's room.

"What do you have there?" Emily perked her head up to inquire.

"Stuff. Stuff from a past life. I can't remember details, but when I hold them, I get these... these visions... these glimmers of things that happened."

"Items, especially those of metals like copper, or gold, can hold lots of energy. You're probably feeling the energy residue of a past life."

"Abigail told me I had powers, but I can't remember what they were."

"I'm sure in time, you'll figure out what they are. Just have patience, Alyson. It took a little while for even Sadie and I to understand our magic and how to control it."

"What do you feel when you hold this boot?" I handed it to Emily and she quickly transformed into a girl. She held the boot into her hand. "It feels like you, only older, and... and more dangerous."

"More dangerous?"

"Yes, there is a hint of dark magic within your blood. In all of your past lives, there is probably one that was not so good. You might've even done evil things."

"I killed a man."

"Yes, that would be considered an evil deed, but not necessarily dark magic."

"No, I mean – I just had a vision as I held this dagger. I killed a man with it."

"Do you know who it was?"

"No. I can't see that."

"Well a dagger that has blood spilled on it will never wash clean, Alyson. Your knife is tainted."

"Tainted?"

"It carries the blood of a person in your past. Like it or not, you're linked with that person."

"So, how do I get rid of it or unlink from him?"

"I'm not sure. Maybe that's something you have to figure out in this life, or..."

"Or what?"

"Or you may have to go back to the past to figure it out."

"You mean, go back into my past life?"

Emelia nodded.

"Who were you in your past lives?" I asked her.

She smiled. "Some things are better left unshared. Just know that I am with you in this one, and I will help you reach your goal."

I looked at the boots.

"Meditate on it. Put the boots on. I'll stay with you."

"Should I hold the dagger?"

"The dagger will have its own memories associated with it, and most certainly I feel you are not ready to face those in your dreams alone. I shall hold onto it for you."

Emelia was rarely wrong. I trusted her. She carried the wisdom of Abigail on a smaller scale. The boots didn't even look to be my size. Still, I inserted my foot into one and then the other, lacing them both up. They were a little snug. I lay back on my bed and closed my eyes.

"Do you really think this will work?"

"It may. It may give you a glimpse of what you're looking for. I'll keep watch over you."

I fell asleep into a lucid dream on the bed. Everything slowed down, including my breath and heart rate. My body felt cold underneath several blankets. Images began to appear in my head.

No sooner had I put on Elisabeth's shoes, I'd stepped into the past. Whether I'd portaled or just entered into a retrocognitive dream I had yet to find out.

I left the room and walked out towards the stairs and descended them. I opened the front door. I saw a man. He resembled Ethan. I reached out to take his hand.

"Jonathan. What are you doing here?"

"Hurry. We don't have much time." I stepped outside. He grabbed my arm and pulled me into the dark alleyway. Looking behind me revealed the scenery had once again changed. A loose cobblestone from the road wobbled under my foot.

I huddled close to Jonathan. "We can't avoid the shadows. We're wanted. There's a bounty on our heads, Jonathan!"

"There are at least a dozen unsolved murders in this town, and I suspect he's wanted just as much as we are!"

"Who is here?"

"I do not know his name. He hides in the shadows. But his eyes, his dark and bird-like eyes are so empty and hollow – it has been said you will die just looking into them."

We peered around the corner of the alleyway. Nestled up against Hremm Nevar was none other than Sadie! This was no longer the 1800's. I felt as though I'd slipped backwards in time even further. What year it was I did not know. Jonathan no longer was with me. My clothing was tattered and the urgency to run from shadow to shadow was present.

"My bride – bring me the book and I will make you a Queen! I will give you powers beyond words!" Sadie looked amused.

I knew who it was. I knew all about him. Hremm Nevar was no match for me. He had powers of mine, powers I wanted back. I paused to let the moment sink in. I looked around me. Again, I'd slipped through time, only this time Sadie was here too, and Hremm Nevar! But how?

I stood outside of a theatre in the alleyway. A playbill lay on the ground. I picked it up. *The Beggar's Three Penny Opera*. The year: 1782.

"Did you enjoy the show?" a man in black asked. He pulled out a jack-knife.

I quickly awoke from my dream in a sweat and gasped. It took several moments to register that I was back in the safety of my home. Who was that?

"Emelia? I was just about to be killed!"

"I know. I am able to enter your dreams, remember? I saw too. I don't know who that was."

How did Sadie portal into the past? "Sadie will betray us again, I am sure of it! This was not just a dream, Emelia, was it?"

"No."

It clicked.

Sadie found the secret room.

Chapter 20

TIME'S SHAKING UP

he arrival of the boots stirred my memory. Glimpses of things I knew in the past and suspected in the future kept popping into my mind. I loved adventure. Having a life full of constant mis-adventures proved to be rewarding for me. Often it led me to exactly what I looked for, even if I didn't know I needed it, or wanted it.

But to see myself narrowly escape a murder was a little more than I'd bargained for. Even more so, I didn't know who it was in that dark alleyway. I only knew of the year – 1782, and that Sadie was there with Hremm Nevar. I questioned if I would have to return to that time to intervene, and if so, would I possibly be a victim?

Why had I slipped backward in time? I knew of Elisabeth Welch, my former self from the 1800's. I thought this shoe belonged to her. Perhaps it was an older shoe belonging to someone else too, someone more than 100 years previous? It was no longer Abigail sending me on these tasks. I had sent myself on this one. I knew I would have to find out more, but at what cost? My life? Who was the girl from the 1700's anyway? An actress? A peasant? A prostitute?

I held the dagger in my hand. It had its own secrets to reveal. Before now, I didn't even know time travel was possible. I didn't know anything about my past lives. I craved more. I sensed there was still much to learn, and with it came an urgency to learn it. My thoughts turned to Sadie.

Sadie had been made aware of the secret room before she ever knew it existed in the past. It was my fault! Unfortunately Sadie's desire for power and greed appeared in my dream – Hremm Nevar had control over her once more.

"A ripple in time has been created. I fear what Sadie may do next. Keep the book safe. It is in the secret room and it must not leave the protection of the house!" Emelia instructed.

"Where is Sadie now?" I asked.

"She has disappeared," Emelia said with a worry laden voice. "I've always known where she was. We are twins. For the first time, she has evaded me, which leads me to believe she may be hiding in a time slip. I do not believe she will stay there if she is after the book. She will return to the secret room. Alyson, we must protect the room and the book."

Mom opened the door to my room without knocking. Emelia didn't have time to change back into a cat. Mom stared at her.

"Oh hello there. Alyson, I didn't know you had a friend over. Getting that math homework done, I hope?"

"Math. Right. We were just studying." I smiled and innocently hoped Mom would leave us alone again.

"Just don't be spending all your time talking about boys. I expect that math homework to be done by supper," she added before closing the door.

"That was close."

"Yes. Twice now I've been caught in my human form. I'm getting careless. I need to focus. Your mother – does she know yet about the secret room?"

"No. I wish I could tell her about you, and Sadie, and Abigail. I wish she knew about it, and her gifts."

"You are forbidden. To do so would mean giving up your own powers. It is up to her to discover it on her own. As with Sadie's example, dire consequences can result if the door is left open and discovered by the unsuspecting. It is only when she is called to it that she will discover its true meaning."

I nodded.

"You'd better attend to that Algebra. I'll go keep watch over the room." She transformed herself back into a grey cat and winked at me.

"Thanks, Emily."

Algebra was difficult to concentrate upon. Even a simple subject would've been a challenge with the tasks I'd recently been sent on. There were much bigger things looming than simple schoolwork. I broke my pencil in half. I needed Mom's help. I felt the presence of something lurking in the near future. Someone I'd seen in my most recent nightmares. Hremm Nevar was back.

Chapter 21

A CRACK IN TIME

A *woof* came from the foot of my bed.

"Shadow, it's not time to go out yet." I looked to the clock. "3 a.m.!? Go back to bed."

"Woof."

"What is it?" Shadow stared outside. I looked out the window. Snow had begun to fall. It lit up the surroundings as moonlight bounced off its white and sparkling surface. It was so pristine, which made it appear calm and clean outside.

But Shadow didn't woof to get my attention for the snowflakes. Shadow woofed because he saw someone run through the snow, just as I did.

Heading down the well trodden forest path that lead to the lake, a girl was running! I was certain it was Sadie. But it was the dryad. She scattered pages over the snow.

"But I'm too tired to go look for them now," I complained. I yanked my blankets over my head.

"Woof."

"Shadow!" I let out a sound resembling a grrr. "Let me sleep! I'm tired already. We can do it in the morning." I looked at the clock again presuming only a few minutes had passed. The clock read "6:15".

I must've had a huge look of panic wave across my face. "How did tha-? What? How can -?"

"Woof woof."

"Oh, two woofs. Fine. I can see this is important. Hang on. Let me get my socks on first."

"Woof."

Shadow ran down the stairs first and to the front door and sat below the hook that held his leash.

"No leash this morning. Just go run and play."

I opened the door to let Shadow out while still assembling all of my body parts into the openings of my winter coat. Shadow did not budge.

"Go on. Go outside already."

He barked.

"Fine. I'm hurrying up. Let's go."

We walked outside in what was a seemingly large amount of new snowfall. It was difficult to walk through. I waded through the path left by the bouncing dog. She headed down towards the lake where I'd seen the dryad.

The dryad had apparently finished her business and moved on, as she was nowhere to be seen, not like I could "see" her with my eyes. Neither were the pages that I'd seen her scattering. Maybe it was only my imagination.

Shadow wandered the trail down to the lake. It was frozen over. I thought of the boat that took us out to the middle, where Hremm Nevar's lair existed. I wondered if any remnants of it remained.

As I stared out into the middle of the lake, a hand burst forth from it, from an area in the center where the ice was too thin to tread upon. The hand held up what appeared to be a set of pages to a book. It disappeared back into the water again, taking the chapters with it.

A voice from the house called out my name. "Alyson? Alyson? Are you outside? Alyson?"

"Yes, Mom," I hollered as I ran back up the snow fallen path. I still had to get ready for school.

As I ran up the path, the moonlight hit the silhouette of a tree I hadn't noticed before. It was shaped like the rune algiz, which means protection. It looked like a hand holding up three fingers. I walked by it more slowly. As I did, I felt a great sense of someone watching over me. I looked around. Shadow was gone!

"Shadow!? Shadow!," I yelled in all directions.

Mom caught up with me near the tree.

"What's wrong?" she asked.

"I can't find Shadow."

We both called out Shadow's name. No response. I felt something was wrong. It wasn't like Shadow to run off. He usually stayed very close to me, literally like a shadow.

"Oh dear. Hope he didn't wander too close to the lake." There was a worried pause in my mother's voice. "Oh my stars, no! We have to go look."

Both Mom and I ran down the path that led to the lake. There sitting on the edge sat a tiny puppy. It simply stared out into the center of the lake.

"No puppy, no!" I commanded.

Shadow looked back at me and barked.

The area at the center of the lake still rippled as the wind hit the open water peeking out from the ice ring. Shadow must've sensed the hand in the lake. I bent down on my knees to get to Shadow's level and clapped my hands.

"Come here boy. It's okay. Come here."

Shadow wagged his tail, but just sat at the edge of the lake. He woofed again and then ran out onto the ice headed toward the center of the lake.

It was horrific.

He fell in.

His paws flailed wildly as he attempted to grip the sides of the ice to climb out, but only managed to chip off more ice in the process. My heart sank and I felt it stop.

"Nooooooooooo!" I screamed. Mom held me back. "No! No! He's just a puppy! No! You can't have him! You can't take him from me! Shadow, no!" Mom held me back as I struggled to break free of her protective grasp. His little black paws gripped helplessly to the edges of the ice. His howls of pain sent shivers down my spine.

"Don't. Don't or you'll go too. Honey, he's gone," she cried.

I had to look away. His howls fell silent. I glanced from the corner of my eye to the center of the lake to see a lone black paw disappear into the ice. He was like a brother to me, and now he was gone.

There was a defining moment of silence. I held her close and let out a cry that could only be mimicked by the sound of a broken heart. I fell to my knees on the shoreline. The sun barely had come up. It approached sunrise.

The silence broke when the sound of birds in flight flocked towards us. I looked back to see the trees perched with hundreds of ravens.

A laugh echoed through the trees. An evil laugh. And then he spoke.

"You called?" Hremm Nevar's voice was unmistakable.

"I didn't call you," I spat up in to the air at the birds.

"Your heart did. You see, I can hear a heart break from the highest realms of the universe," he mocked. "It is music to my ears," he said with a sinister laugh.

The birds terrified me, but I did not respond to him. I looked out to the center of the lake.

"Shadow," I whispered. "Wait for me. Next time you'll wear a leash, I promise."

I looked up at the birds. She stared up at them too, but did not hear the voice of Hremm Nevar.

"Now I understand," she spoke to me while staring up at them.

"Now you understand what?"

"Now I understand why you told me not to paint those ugly birds. You see, I do listen to you," she said with a smile.

"You're brilliant! Mom go paint a picture of the lake, only make sure you paint the lake in the summertime."

She nodded.

"Run. You must do it now!"

I'd never commanded my own mother to do anything before, but she must've sensed the importance and immediacy. If she never realized she had a gift when she painted before, she did now.

"Paint, Mom, paint!" I chanted.

Hremm Nevar laughed. "Very clever. You should be more careful who you do magic around. Others are taking notes," he taunted. I wondered whom he referred to.

From out of the trees fell missing pages. I scurried about collecting them, like a squirrel collecting acorns. The sound of ice cracking on the lake startled me.

From the center of the lake sprang the hand, as it had before, but instead of a text, it held a puppy. The puppy was lifeless. The papers I'd collected fell from my hands and without thought, I found myself walking towards the hand holding Shadow.

My feet walked along the top of the ice until I neared the center of the lake. I stopped and looked at the rising sun's reflection on the ice. As it grew larger and brighter with the rising sun, I noticed something else had happened. I looked around on the outskirts of the lake. Blots of colourful flowers had instantly bloomed. A loud crackling sound came from underneath my feet.

"Mom," almost silently the word left my lips before I fell through the ice too.

I treaded through the icy water, watching the shoreline of the lake thawing into warmer water and coming closer. My body shook uncontrollably. Hyperthermia was setting in.

Mom. Hurry. Paint faster.

As I trembled, before me she'd painted a small grassy island. I treaded quickly to it, noticing as I did so, the water around me got warmer.

I sat upon the warm grass and felt the warmth of summer just over the lake. The surrounding trees stayed covered in snow.

I calmed my breath and looked around. The hand was gone! Shadow... was gone too.

I looked down to the grass, unsure and alone.

"Woof!"

Quickly, I turned behind me. There sat Shadow, with a red leash dangling from his mouth. He dropped it on the ground in front of me.

"Woof."

I responded back to him. "Shadow! Woof to you too! It's good to see you boy!" I threw my arms around his neck and hugged him.

My mom emerged on the side of the forest. She was dressed in her winter clothes. I felt her radiant smile when she saw her creation, and that we were both alive.

The crackling sound appeared again. Ice formed in parts of the lake.

"Time to go," I said to Shadow.

Mom's painting gift had the ability to cast the spell, but lacked cohesiveness. Still, it worked when it needed to. Shadow was alive and I had the missing pages.

Shadow and I ran to shore and stood next to Mom. We all stared at the center of the lake. It had refrozen and the tiny grass island we'd sat upon only moments before, had disappeared.

I clipped the leash onto Shadow's collar and scooped the puppy into my arms. I had the missing chapter. I only had to replace them in the book.

Hremm Nevar's laughter echoed throughout the forest. "It is too late – I have won!" he taunted.

A blast of wind hit my face as the force of a thousand birds flew off. I looked to Mom feeling overwhelmed and defeated. "What did he mean? It's too late. Could it be?"

Chapter 22

PROPHECY

A book can take you anywhere – to a place only in your mind – whereas watching a movie, everyone is forced to experience the scene at the same time – and in the same way. In a book, no one can read what you're reading; no one can read your mind or see the scenes as they unfold. Discovering you have a gift is a lot like opening a new book. You never really know what awaits until you start to turn the page.

I watched my mother as she discovered she had a gift, a gift of saving lives and healing, all through her amazing vision. She painted her dreams and her dreams became reality, even if only for a few sacred moments.

I cuddled Shadow in my arms as I walked down the stairs for breakfast. A heavy smell of burnt toast littered the air, mixed with the earthy scent of coffee. "Mom?" I called out. There was no answer.

I wandered into her paint studio. Spilt pots of paint splattered abstract images on the floor, the colours blending into a myriad of rainbow swirls and splots. "Mom?" I called out once again. She had her back to me in a chair, paintbrush in hand. She did not turn around to face me, but only continued to stare at a painting still fresh with paint.

I placed my hand on her shoulder and she gasped. She had been in a trance. We both looked at the canvas.

"Who is she?" I asked.

"I'm not sure. I dreamt of her, and in my dream, she asked me to paint her."

"She asked you to paint her?" I questioned. I heralded at the thought perhaps she talked with Abigail, or even Emelia, but this lady in the painting was someone completely different. She held a blue wisp in her hand. A sea of horses galloped behind her in the waves and her dress became a blanket of stars.

"Yes. I cannot explain it. Just as I cannot explain the inspiration for my other paintings. They come to me in dreams; in visions."

"Do you know who this is?"

"Yes."

"Who is she?"

"She is my mother."

"Your mother?"

"She is your mother too."

We both paused and stared at the painting.

She spoke again. "Yesterday I learned everything I believed to be real, I had created. I created my own destiny. My paintings, I knew about them long before, but did not realize the magnitude of the effect it would have. I did not know I could save a life."

"You have saved more than just one life." I hugged her.

"The woman, this woman, here in the painting… she has been visiting me in my dreams since I was just a little girl. Today, I sat down at the canvas of the frozen lake. As soon as my brush touched the canvas, it was as though my hand was no longer my own, but rather an extension of myself – a higher self. And I drew her. She almost looks alive."

"She may very well be," I answered with a smile.

"I found the room," she said hastily as she spun around in her chair. "I found it the other day, just after you'd left for school."

I hesitated a moment. "Which room?"

She looked me square in the eye. "The room at the top of the stairs. There is a secret room hidden inside of the linen cupboard," she whispered, almost as if for protection in case someone unseen listened to our private conversation.

I wondered what she'd seen. I didn't want to open my mouth and reveal too much. "Oh?" I played dumb. "There is a room in a linen closet? How... umm... interesting."

"There was a pedestal in the middle of the room. It almost looked like a book was meant to be there."

"Wait, a book? Did you say a book?"

"Yes. But there wasn't a book. It was just funny seeing an empty pedestal in the middle of this curious attic room all cluttered with antiques. It would make a nice observatory though. It has a lovely skylight in the ceiling. Funny how you can't see it from outside. Must be the angle."

"The book is gone?!"

"What book? Honey, why are you going on about some book? Was it a yearbook?"

My jaw dropped. I barely answered her before fleeing the room. "Mom, I'll be right back."

I dashed out of the studio and ran up two flights of stairs to get to the top floor. I crawled under the table and depressed the wall until it opened to reveal its secret passageway. Quickly I rushed to the top of the stairs and turned the corner. The cupboard door was ajar!

"Oh no!"

I approached it with caution. A cold breeze passed over my naked feet. My fingertips glided along the edge of the door as I peeked inside. I entered cautiously.

Mom was right!

The book was gone!

Only a black feather left in its place.

The sacred book had been stolen – the security of the secret room compromised.

Sadie stepped into the room. She grimaced and threw me across the room with a wave of her hand.

"I'm sorry, Alyson. But he promised me great power in trade for the book. Most notably, your powers!"

My powers? I could barely stand. Her magic was incredibly intense in the secret room, almost doubly so what I'd seen her do in the past.

"Sadie, I – I saw you. I saw you with him." I looked at her more closely. Faint images of her undead self appeared to flicker before me, as though she was time-shifting between her two selves. She appeared disturbed and teetering on the edge of madness. "What's happened to you?"

She grimaced again and fired a bolt of blue fire lightning from her hand at me. It knocked me into a wall.

"Of course you did!" she said with a snicker. "It's too bad I have your powers."

I attempted to stand, but could not. I backed up against the wall and watched as Sadie stood at the altar's center, laughing and gazing at me with a cold death stare. She held the staff in her hands — *the* staff — Hremm Nevar's staff!

How did she get it back? Abigail destroyed it… she can summon him with it! She's in the secret room!

Wind rushed through the secret room as my head filled with dismay and confusion. Sadie's laughter reverberated against every angle. She let out a banshee cry and her eyes turned black! Darkness consumed her. The stained-glass window burst and shattered into a thousand tiny pieces. The room was no longer a secret. I turned my head to see giant flapping black wings thundering towards me.

"He's coming for *you* now, Alyson."

… To be continued…

BOOKS BY KRISTIN GROULX:

The mis-adventures of Alyson Bell
Young Adult Paranormal Romance Series:

Book One: *The Ghost of Colby Drive*
(ISBN 978-0-9811315-0-4, July 2007)

Alyson Bell, new to the rural town of Hollow Creek: a town rumoured to be haunted by a ghostly spirit and a cat with more than the usual nine lives. Alyson unwillingly transitions into her new life, facing everyday teenage obstacles (bosoms and boyfriends), and hurdling over supernatural mysteries only *she* is predestined to encounter. Does one girl have what it takes to piece together the myriad of clues left behind in her century-old house to end a *cat*-astrophic curse, vanquish an evil soul-stealing vampire and still have time for a relationship with her new boyfriend, all before the next full moon?

Book Two: *The Curse of the Moonless Knight*
(ISBN 978-0-9811315-1-1, August 2008)

It is the season of Samhain, also celebrated as Hallowe'en. The crisp of Fall is in the air. Spirits are amiss in the town of Hollow Creek when a portal that should've stayed closed, is accidentally opened. A medieval knight, misplaced in time, links sixteen year-old Alyson to an extraordinary discovery about herself, and her family. Embarking on a quest for knowledge, Alyson learns that sometimes in this magical world, you have to close your eyes... *to see*. And in order to forgive, you must first open your heart.

Book Three: The Oracle of the Missing Dryad
(ISBN 978-0-9811315-2-8, September 2009)

Sometimes the pages just write themselves... as though, the spirit of the wood still lives between the text, dancing between pages and weaving magic. Alyson Bell meets a tree dryad who helps Alyson on her latest adventure, that is, until the book the spirit is hiding inside of gets stolen and it's up to Alyson to travel through time to find her! For she holds the key that unlocks both the past and the future, and her prophecy is revealed.

Book Four: The Door of the Thousand Keys
(ISBN 978-0-9811315-4-2, October 2010)

Book Five: The Crystal Goddess and the Wish Keeper
(ISBN 978-0-9811315-3-5, November 2011)

Book Six: (Secret Title)
(November 2012)

A bit of lore from days ago

O! Mistletoe! Mistletoe, also known as the golden bough was held sacred by both the Celtic Druids and the Norseman. Once called Allheal, used in folk medicine to cure many ills. North American Indians used it for toothache, measles and dog bites. Today the plant is still used medicinally, though only in skilled hands...it's a powerful plant.

It was also the plant of peace in Scandinavian antiquity. If enemies met by chance beneath it in a forest, they laid down their arms and maintained a truce until the next day.

Mistletoe was used by the Druid priesthood in a very special ceremony ... five days after the New Moon following winter solstice, to be precise. The Druid priests would cut mistletoe from a holy oak tree with a golden sickle. The branches had to be caught before they touched the ground.

Celts believed this parasitic plant held the soul of the host tree.

Although many sources say that kissing under the mistletoe is a purely English custom, there's another, more charming explanation for its origin that extends back into Norse mythology. It's the story of a loving, if overprotective, mother.

The tradition of kissing under the mistletoe may have its roots in Norse legend. Frigga, goddess of love had a son named Balder.

Because of a dream he had, she became alarmed and sought to protect him from harm from every living creature and plant, that he could not be harmed by anything on or under the earth. Mistletoe did not grow on or under the earth, but on trees. The evil god Loki knew this and prepared a poison arrow with it with which Balder was killed. After three days Frigga was able to restore her son to life and from then on, it is said she kissed everyone who passed under the mistletoe and decreed that it stood for life and love from then on.

In England the tradition of mistletoe goes back before the birth of Christ. Mistletoe was revered by the Druids, and mistletoe that grew on an oak was considered to have magical qualities. The plant was a symbol of fertility, as it remained green even as the deciduous trees it grew upon appeared to freeze in winter's icy grip.

The plant continued to be endowed by superstition with mystical and healing properties throughout medieval times. The tradition of hanging the plant in doorways began in England and it was considered good luck as well as a love charm. Over time this tradition included kissing under the mistletoe with the superstition that a girl who wasn't kissed would not be married within the coming year.

Our story begins on the Winter Solstice, the shortest day of the year, (usually around Dec. 21) also known as Yule. It is on this day that we celebrate the Goddess giving birth to the God, a reminder that with death comes rebirth. It is a joyous celebration of family and friends, of peace and love and positive energy.

It came upon the midnight clear,
That glorious song of old,
From angels bending near the earth,
To touch their harps of gold;
"Peace on the earth, good will to men,
From Heaven's all gracious King."
The world in solemn stillness lay,
To hear the angels sing.

Still through the cloven skies they come
With peaceful wings unfurled,
And still their heavenly music floats
O'er all the weary world;
Above its sad and lowly plains,
They bend on hovering wing,
And ever over its Babel sounds
The blessèd angels sing.

Yet with the woes of sin and strife
The world has suffered long;
Beneath the angel strain have rolled
Two thousand years of wrong;
And man, at war with man, hears not
The love-song which they bring;
O hush the noise, ye men of strife
And hear the angels sing.

And ye, beneath life's crushing load,
Whose forms are bending low,
Who toil along the climbing way
With painful steps and slow,
Look now! for glad and golden hours
Come swiftly on the wing.
O rest beside the weary road,
And hear the angels sing!

For lo! the days are hastening on,
By prophet-bards foretold,
When with the ever circling years
Comes round the age of gold;
When peace shall over all the earth
Its ancient splendors fling,
And the whole world send back the song
Which now the angels sing.

Words: Edmund H. Sears, in the **Christian Register** (Boston, Massachusetts: December 29, 1849), volume 28, number 52, page 206. Sears is said to have written these words at the request of his friend, W. P. Lunt, a minister in Quincy, Massachusetts; the hymn was first sung at the 1849
Sunday School Christmas celebration.

Music: Carol, Richard S. Willis, **Church Chorals and Choir Studies**, 1850. Alternate tune: Noel, arranged by Arthur S. Sullivan, 1871

www.ingramcontent.com/pod-product-compliance
Lightning Source LLC
LaVergne TN
LVHW091538060526
838200LV00036B/656